Cecilia didn't want to be protected, but sometimes she wanted to be soothed.

She didn't need anyone to fight her fights, but sometimes she needed someone to dress her wounds. Literally. Figuratively.

Brady did that. Just...by being him.

His fingers tightened in her hair, and the kiss that had begun as soft and lazy heated, sharpened. Something ignited deep inside of her, a hunger she hadn't really thought could exist inside of her. It had certainly never leaped to life before.

But now.... Now she wanted to sink into that heat and that unfurling desperation. It was new and it was heady and it was better than all that had come before.

ISOLATED THREAT

Nicole Helm

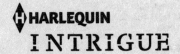

HARLEQUIN
INTRIGUE

For those who've learned to ask for help.

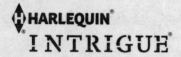

Recycling programs
for this product may
not exist in your area.

ISBN-13: 978-1-335-13655-8

Isolated Threat

Harlequin Enterprises ULC
22 Adelaide St. West, 40th Floor
Toronto, Ontario M5H 4E3, Canada
www.Harlequin.com

Printed in U.S.A.

Nicole Helm grew up with her nose in a book and the dream of one day becoming a writer. Luckily, after a few failed career choices, she gets to follow that dream—writing down-to-earth contemporary romance and romantic suspense. From farmers to cowboys, Midwest to *the* West, Nicole writes stories about people finding themselves and finding love in the process. She lives in Missouri with her husband and two sons and dreams of someday owning a barn.

Books by Nicole Helm

Harlequin Intrigue

A Badlands Cops Novel

South Dakota Showdown
Covert Complication
Backcountry Escape
Isolated Threat

Carsons & Delaneys: Battle Tested

Wyoming Cowboy Marine
Wyoming Cowboy Sniper
Wyoming Cowboy Ranger
Wyoming Cowboy Bodyguard

Carsons & Delaneys

Wyoming Cowboy Justice
Wyoming Cowboy Protection
Wyoming Christmas Ransom

Stone Cold Texas Ranger
Stone Cold Undercover Agent
Stone Cold Christmas Ranger

Harlequin Superromance

A Farmers' Market Story

All I Have
All I Am
All I Want

Falling for the New Guy
Too Friendly to Date
Too Close to Resist

Visit the Author Profile page at Harlequin.com.

CAST OF CHARACTERS

Cecilia Mills—Tribal police officer who is protecting her friend's son; niece to Duke Knight, who took her in after her parents died when she was a child.

Brady Wyatt—The middle Wyatt brother, a sheriff's deputy who was shot in the shoulder and is still struggling to recover. Agrees to help Cecilia protect her friend's baby.

Layla—Cecilia's friend who is suffering from postpartum depression and asks Cecilia to hide her son from his biological father.

Mak—Layla and Elijah's six-month-old son.

Elijah Jones—Mak's father, member of the Sons of the Badlands.

Felicity Harrison—Cecilia's foster sister, engaged to Gage Wyatt.

Gage Wyatt—Brady's twin brother. Also a sheriff's deputy.

Grandma Pauline Reaves—The Wyatt brothers' grandmother who took them in after they escaped their father's gang.

Rachel Knight—Felicity's cousin, a teacher on the reservation who stays with Cecilia sometimes.

Liza Dean-Wyatt—Cecilia's foster sister, married to the eldest Wyatt brother.

Chapter One

In the dark of his apartment, Brady Wyatt considered getting drunk.

It wasn't something he typically considered doing. He stayed away from extremes. If he drank alcohol, it was usually two beers tops. He'd never smoked a cigarette or taken a drug that wasn't expressly legal.

He was a good man. He believed in right and wrong. He believed wholeheartedly that he was smarter, better and stronger than his father, who was currently being transferred to a maximum-security federal prison, thanks to a number of charges, including attempted murder.

When Brady thought of his twin brother nearly dying at Ace's hands, it made him want to get all the more drunk.

Brady wished he could believe Ace Wyatt would no longer be a threat. His father wasn't superhuman or supernatural, but sometimes…no matter what Brady told himself was possible, it felt like Ace Wyatt would always have a choke hold around his neck.

Once he could go back to work, things would be fine. Dark thoughts and this sense of impending doom would go away once he could get out there and do his job again.

The fact he'd been shot was a setback, but he'd taken his role as sheriff's deputy for Valiant County, South Dakota, seriously enough to know being hurt, or even killed, in the line of duty was more than possible.

He'd been shot helping save his soon-to-be sister-in-law. There was no shame or regret in that.

But the fact the wound had gotten infected, didn't seem to want to heal in any of the normal ways no matter what doctors he saw, left him frustrated and often spiraling into dark corners of his mind he had no business going.

When someone knocked on his apartment door, relief swept through him. A relief that made him realize how much the darkness had isolated him.

Maybe he should go stay out at his grandmother's ranch. Let Grandma Pauline shove food at him and let his brother Dev grouse at him. Being alone wasn't doing him any favors, and he was not a man who indulged in weakness.

He looked through the peephole, and was more than a little shocked to see Cecilia Mills standing there.

Any relief he'd felt at having company evaporated. Cecilia was not a welcome presence in his life right now, and hadn't been since New Year's Eve when she'd decided to kiss him, full on the mouth.

Cecilia had grown up with the Knights, on the neighboring ranch to his grandmother's. Duke and Eva Knight's niece had been part of the fabric of Brady's life since he'd come to live with Grandma Pauline at the age of eleven—after his oldest brother had helped him escape their father's gang, the Sons of the Badlands.

While Brady had been friends with all the Knight girls, Cecilia was the one who'd always done her level best to irritate him. Not always on purpose either. They were just…diametrically opposed. Despite her job as a tribal police officer on the nearby reservation, Cecilia bent rules all the time. She saw gray when he saw black, and even darker gray when he saw white. She was complicated and they didn't agree on much of anything.

Except that their fundamental function in life was to help people. Which, he supposed, was what had made them good friends despite all their arguments.

Until she'd kissed him and ruined it all. She hadn't even *tried* to pass it off as a joke when he'd expressed his horror.

Still, he opened the door to her, even if he couldn't muster a polite smile.

She was soaked to the bone, carrying a bundle of blankets. The blankets let out a little mewling cry and Cecilia shoved her way inside.

Not just blankets. A baby.

"Close the door," she ordered roughly.

He raised an eyebrow but did as he was told, if only because there was panic underneath that stern order.

Her long black hair was pulled back in the braid she usually wore for work, but she wasn't wearing her tribal police officer uniform. Her jeans and T-shirt hung loose and wet and her tennis shoes were muddy and battered. Even with the panic on her face, and the casual clothes, there was an air about her that screamed *cop*.

He should know.

"What's all this?"

Goose bumps pricked visibly along her arms and she quickly began unbundling the baby. It was warm outside, even with the all-day rain, so he had the air conditioner running. He moved to turn it off.

"You got anything dry for him?" she asked.

Brady wanted explanations, but he could see just how wet they both were. So, he walked into his room and rummaged around for dry clothes for Cecilia, and a few things to wrap around a small infant. He grabbed some towels from the bathroom and headed back to his living room.

He handed the towel to her first. She knelt on the floor, placing the baby gently on the rug. She spoke softly to the child, unwrapping the wet layers, and even the diaper. Brady winced a little as she wrapped the baby's bare butt in the towel he'd given her, rather than a new, dry diaper, though she didn't appear to have any baby supplies.

"You need to get out of your wet clothes too," he insisted once the baby was taken care of.

She looked up at him, an arch look as if he was coming on to her.

Heat infused him, an embarrassment he didn't know what to do with. He did not *blush*, being a grown man. He was probably just feverish from this damn infection he couldn't kick. Again.

"I'm not going to jump you," Cecilia said in that flippant way of hers that always set his teeth on edge. "That ship has sailed. So unclench."

He had never appreciated Cecilia's irreverence for the rules of life. Or at least, *his* rules of life. One of which was nothing romantic between him and any of the Knight girls. Maybe some of his brothers had crossed that line, somehow made it work, but Brady had his rules. If there'd been a brief, confusing second on New Year's Eve when Cecilia's surprise kiss had made him wonder why, it was a moment of weakness he wouldn't indulge.

Cecilia didn't follow the letter of the law. She often advocated for wrong as much as right. She had *kissed* him. On the mouth. Very much against his will.

Then had had the nerve to laugh when he'd lectured her.

"Just go to my room and change," he grumbled. "I'll watch…" He gestured at the baby.

She looked back at the wriggling infant she was crouching over. Pain clouded her eyes, and fear was etched into her face.

"This is Mak." She stroked his cheek with the gentleness of a mother, but Brady knew Cecilia had not secretly been pregnant or given birth to a child. He saw her too often for that to be possible.

He sighed, sympathy warring with irritation. "What's going on, Cecilia?"

CECILIA COULD FEEL the shivering start to spread. It had been hot outside in the rainstorm, but Brady's apartment was cold. Pretty soon her teeth would chatter, no matter how hard she fought against it.

And she would fight against it. Showing weakness in front of Brady Wyatt wasn't something she could afford right now. She had to be in charge if this was ever going to work. If she was ever going to convince by-the-book Brady to go along with it.

"I'll go change. You can leave him there or pick him up. He can roll over though, so keep an eye on him."

She grabbed the stuff he'd brought out, helped herself to his room, and then once the door was closed, slumped against it.

She'd been a tribal police officer for seven years. She'd been afraid, truly afraid for her life. She had struggled to understand the right thing to do in the face of laws that weren't always *fair*. It was hard, stressful, at times painful work, and she intimately knew fear.

But this was new. Bigger and different.

She didn't want to die, so she feared for her own life when she had to at work. But she'd also accepted that she *would* die to save someone. That was why she'd gone into law enforcement, or at least something she'd accepted as she'd taken on a badge.

Now she had a *specific* someone. A tiny, defenseless baby. Poor little Mak. He didn't deserve the stress and panic of being on the run, and yet she didn't know what else to do. If Elijah got a hold of him…

Cecilia shook her head.

She needed help. She needed…

God, she did not need Brady Wyatt, but she didn't have any other viable options in the moment. And the moment was all there was.

It was that lack of options that forced her to move. She stripped off her wet clothes, then put on the dry, too-big ones that were Brady's. She paused at that. Brady had worn these clothes on his body.

And washed them, you moron.

She couldn't help the fact she had the hots for Brady. Couldn't help that the New Year's Eve kiss hadn't helped dissipate them any. Luckily the memory of his stern lecture afterward always made her laugh.

He was just so *uptight*. He drove her crazy. Yet, there was this physical thing that also drove her a different kind of crazy. She believed deep down it was just her dualistic nature. Of course she'd be attracted to someone whose personality made her want to pull her hair out.

That was her lot in life.

But that lot was way in the background now. Her only concern was finding a way to protect Mak. Cecilia had been trying to help her friend Layla through postpartum depression for the better part of six months, but a suicide attempt had landed Layla in the hospital with the state preparing to take Mak away.

Layla had begged Cecilia to hide him. The state would only take him to his father, who was rising in the ranks with the Sons of the Badlands.

The fact Ace Wyatt's gang had begun to infiltrate the reservation Cecilia worked and lived on, the place she'd been born, filled her with a fury that scared her.

So, she'd focus on this. Keeping Mak safe until Layla was given a clean bill of mental health.

Elijah had already threatened to take Mak, maybe more than once. Layla wasn't always forthcoming with what went down with Elijah, since there was still a part of Layla who believed she could save the man she loved from the wrong he was doing.

Cecilia didn't believe. She knew the world was gray—that black and white were illusions made by people who had the privilege to see the world that way—but anyone who moved up the ranks in the Sons was too far gone to change for the better.

She would save the innocent baby who'd had the

misfortune of a terrible father and an emotionally abused mother.

She'd been that baby, more or less, and her aunt and uncle had saved her. Showed her love and kindness and taken her in when her mother had died. She'd been six years old. Aunt Eva was gone too now, but she still had Uncle Duke, and the four other women he'd raised who were her sisters regardless of biological ties.

Cecilia tied the sweatpants tight around her waist. They were too long by far, but she cuffed the ends, then did the same with the sleeves of the sweatshirt. She took the bundle of wet clothes with her as she stepped back into the living room.

She stopped short. Brady held Mak, cradled easily in his good arm. Brady wore a T-shirt, so she could see a hint of the bandage that was on his opposite shoulder.

Recovery from the gunshot wound he'd received when saving Felicity had been complicated.

There were six Wyatt brothers, any of whom she could get help from. Easier help. All of them understood, to a point, you had to bend some rules to save people from the Sons.

Brady was the one who didn't, or wouldn't, accept that. He was also the one who currently couldn't work. Who lived alone. Who could hide a baby.

Elijah might think to look at the Wyatt Ranch for Mak, but he wouldn't think to look into Brady individually. Not at first anyway. Not while she came up with a plan.

"Can I throw these in your dryer?"

Brady inclined his head, gently swaying Mak's body back and forth as if Brady had any practice with calming babies.

She'd spent some time in Brady's apartment. Not much. They'd all helped him out here over the past two months, trying to give a hand with chores that might hurt his shoulder. She'd come over with Felicity and Gage one night and made him dinner. She'd delivered some food courtesy of Grandma Pauline a few weeks ago when he'd been doing laundry, and despite how little she wanted to be alone with him when everything about him made her body *react*, she'd insisted on helping him move the clothes from the washer to the dryer.

She did so now, tossing her own clothes in the dryer. She wouldn't have time for them to get completely dry, but it would help. Hopefully the rain would stop so it wouldn't be a completely futile gesture.

She hesitated going back into the living room. Much as she wanted Mak in her own arms where his warm weight gave her a settled purpose, she knew she couldn't go back to Brady without a clear sense of what she was going to say.

She'd practiced on the way here. She'd just go with that. *Brady. I need your help. I know you won't approve, but you're the only one who can keep this*

*innocent child safe and away from the Sons. I know
you'll do the right thing.*

Simple. To the point.

But as Cecilia stood on the threshold of his small,
stark living room, watching a big man holding a tiny
baby, she could only say one thing.

"His father is a member of the Sons."

Brady's expression did that thing that had always
fascinated her. It didn't chill. It didn't heat. It was
like something inside of him clicked off and he went
perfectly blank.

She envied that ability.

"His mother is in the hospital," she continued.
"The state is going to award him to his father. I can't
let that happen."

"It's not up to you, Cecilia."

He said it so coolly, so *calm*. She wanted to
scream, maybe give him a good punch like he'd once
taught her to do when she'd been thirteen and a boy
at school was bothering her.

But rage and punching never got through to Brady
Wyatt. So, she had to be harsh. As uncompromis-
ing as he always was. "Would you send this baby to
survive *your* childhood?" Because Brady had spent
eleven years stuck with the Sons, surviving his father—the leader of that terrible gang.

There was a flicker of something in his eyes, but
his words and the delivery didn't change. "He isn't
Ace's son."

"He could be," Cecilia returned, trying to match

his lack of emotion and failing. "Ace is gone. Elijah is trying to move up, take over. He's recruiting people at the rez at a rapid rate."

"Elijah Jones," Brady said flatly.

The fact Brady knew him didn't soothe Cecilia's nerves any. "Yes. You know him?"

"Of him," Brady replied, still so blank and unreachable. "He has a record." Brady's gaze lifted from the baby to her. "The state wouldn't put a child with someone who—"

"You know what? Forget it." God, he infuriated her. After everything he'd seen as a police officer, everything he'd survived as a boy, he could believe the state would do the right thing. She marched toward him. "I don't need your help. I don't need you and your rigid, ignorant belief in a system that does not work. Hand him over." She held out her arms.

But Brady simply angled his body, keeping Mak just out of her reach. "No," he said firmly.

Chapter Two

Brady had seen Cecilia angry plenty of times. She was a woman of extremes. Completely calm and chill, or…this. Fury all but pumping off her in waves. If he hadn't been holding a baby, he was certain she would have decked him. Possibly right in the gunshot wound.

"You brought him here for a reason," he said in a tone of voice he'd learned and used over the years as a police officer. Calm, but not condescending. Authoritative without being demanding. It often soothed.

Not with Cecilia. "Yes, and boy was it a stupid reason," she returned through gritted teeth. He could practically see the wheels in her head turning as she tried to figure out how to get the baby away from him without hurting Mak.

"Why don't you calm down and—"

She bunched her fist and he winced because he'd made a serious tactical error in telling her to calm down.

"I swear to God I will—"

The baby in his arm began to cry. Brady blinked down at the little bundle wiggling against his arm. He'd dealt with babies before—not often, but he'd held them. Calmed a few after a traffic accident or during a domestic case. Babies weren't new or strange to him.

But little Mak was so tiny. His face wrinkled in distress as he cried, clearly disturbed by the sound of raised voices. He had a patch of dark hair, and spindly little limbs that reminded Brady of a movie alien.

Cecilia held out her arms, gave Brady a warning look, but Brady simply bounced the baby until he calmed, nestled closer. There was something comforting about the weight of him. Something real and…heavy, even though the child was light. Brady had been adrift for weeks, and holding Mak felt like a weight tethering him to shore.

Cecilia frowned, her forehead wrinkling in much the same way Mak's had. But she didn't argue with him any more. There was a kind of anguish on her face that had his heart twisting.

Brady nodded to the couch. "Sit. Tell me the whole story," he ordered quietly.

"I don't want to sit," she returned, petulantly if he had to describe it.

She would not have appreciated that characterization. She folded her arms across her chest and began to pace.

She was tall and slender and like a lot of the female cops he knew, played down everything that made her look too feminine. Her hair was simple—straight, black, braided. She wore no makeup, and the jeans and T-shirt she'd shown up in were on the baggy side, as if she might have to put her Kevlar on underneath.

Cecilia could flip the switch when she wanted to. Put on a dress, do up her face in that magical way women seemed to have—like she had on New Year's Eve, all glitter and smoke and fun. She even seemed to enjoy it. Or maybe she'd just enjoyed knocking him off his axis.

With Cecilia, he'd bet on the latter.

"His mother's in the hospital. She…" Cecilia hugged herself tighter, then finally sat on his couch. "She's one of my oldest friends on the rez. She's been wrapped up in Elijah Jones for years now. I couldn't come out and say he was bad news, you know?" She looked up at him, an uncomfortable amount of imploring in her eyes. "If you say they're bad, it only makes some people want to hold on even more. Fix them even more. Some people don't understand that not everyone is fixable."

Brady nodded. He'd worked enough domestic cases to know that people of both sexes were often blinded by what they thought was love. Enough to believe they could change the worst in someone else.

Cecilia seemed to find some relief in his understanding. "So, I tried to be subtle. I tried to make it more about her. What she should have. What she *could* have if she only gave up on holding herself back." Cecilia shook her head. "Anyway, she was ecstatic when she got pregnant. Elijah stuck around more. He had plans. But they all involved the Sons." Her tone turned to acid. "Layla had the baby, and Elijah told her he'd be back once the kid was out of diapers so he could take him. *Make* him."

Cecilia popped back up onto her feet. "Take him. As if that boy was a peach that had to ripen before he ate it. Take him, as if he had any right." She shook her head vigorously. "Layla had already been struggling a bit, but that really sent her over the edge. I helped out, but I urged her to talk to her doctor. Something wasn't right. Finally I took her down to her doctor myself and wouldn't leave until she told someone how she was feeling. They said it was post-partum depression."

"Common enough."

"Sure. Sure. Since then I've done my level best to help her out. To do what I could to help Mak. I took her to her appointments, but we had a hard time scheduling them. Her insurance is terrible and she was already struggling financially. She didn't have any supportive family, and I tried to be that for her, but…"

"You're only one person, Cecilia." It came out gentler than he'd intended, and the look of anguish she sent him made his chest too tight.

She collapsed back onto the couch. "One person or ten, it doesn't seem to matter. The night I came to the hospital to talk to Felicity and Gage, that night you were shot? She took a bunch of pills. She called me. Told me, so I called an ambulance and it got there in time, but—"

"You know better than to blame yourself."

"Do I?" she snapped.

"You should," he replied, keeping his voice gentle even though he wanted to snap right back. She should know better, and she shouldn't be sitting here making him feel sorry for her. She didn't want his pity any more than he wanted to give it.

"Yeah, well *should* can bite me. I do blame myself, and I will," Cecilia replied with a sneer, though it quickly faded. "I also know if it weren't for me, she would have had no one to call and she would have died. So, maybe it evens out. I don't know. They let me see her and she begged me to take Mak. He was with a neighbor and Layla didn't trust the woman not to hand him over to the state or Elijah." Cecilia blew out a breath. "She just needs help. She needs to get through this. She won't if Mak is with Elijah. Or gets shipped off into foster care."

"Cecilia, there are laws and rules and—"

"I had to. I *have* to do this for her. I know you only care about your precious laws and rules, but—"

"Those precious laws and rules are the difference between people like us and people like Elijah." And Ace. Though he didn't say that aloud, he had the uncomfortable feeling she heard it anyway.

"Except when those laws are going to hurt an innocent baby," Cecilia insisted. "If they give Mak to

Elijah, being abused by the Sons is all that boy has to hope for. Is that what you want?"

Of course it wasn't. He didn't want that for anyone. It wasn't that he thought the law was infallible, that people didn't fall through the cracks of it. No rule could possibly apply to everyone in every situation, but this wasn't so much about following the letter of the law as it was about consequences.

"We could both get fired for this. You far more than me, but it risks both of our badges. We are sworn to uphold and protect the law, even when we don't agree with it."

She closed her eyes, then buried her face in her hands. Brady was rendered speechless and frozen in place for a good minute as Cecilia began to cry.

He'd never seen her cry before. She'd broken her arm falling out of a tree when she'd been thirteen and she hadn't cried. She'd yelled and cursed a blue streak, but she hadn't actually cried. At least not while he'd stayed with her and Gage had run to get help.

"Stop that," was all he could think to say.

She looked up at him dolefully, her face tearstained and blotchy. "You're such a comforting soul, Brady," she replied, her voice scratchy.

He didn't know what to say to that, since usually he *could* comfort people. Usually he knew what to say, how to calm and soothe so the work could be done. If she was anyone else he would have sat next to her on the couch and patted her shoulder, or leg or something. He would have known what to do with her tears.

But when it came to Cecilia, all those options seemed dangerous, and he didn't want to figure out why. He wanted to keep his distance.

"I'm sorry," she said on a sigh.

"You don't have to apologize for crying."

She rolled her eyes, wiping her cheeks with her palms. "I'm not sorry for crying. I'm sorry because I shouldn't have brought this to your doorstep. It's just, I had to think of the place Elijah would be least likely to look for Mak. He's going to suspect I had something to do with Mak's disappearance—Layla's neighbor will no doubt tell him who took him even though I bribed her not to. So, he'd know to look at the ranches, and I thought Nina and Liza made them too obvious," she said, speaking of her foster sisters who each had a child in her care—Liza her young half sister and Nina her daughter. "But you're just a bachelor in an apartment."

"Just a bachelor in an apartment," Brady repeated, surprised at how much that appraisal hurt.

"You know what I mean. Besides, you're hurt. He'd think less of you because of it. He'd think I'd want Mak with someone…"

"Who could actually protect him." That feeling of everything that had gone wrong since the gunshot wound settled deeper. He nodded toward his bad shoulder. "I *can't* protect him."

Cecilia stood again. Though the traces of tears

were still on her face, there was something powerful about the way she stood, the way she angled him with a doleful look. "I'd take an injured Wyatt over just about anyone else. You'll protect just fine."

Brady didn't want that kind of responsibility thrust upon him when he was so... Things weren't right inside of him, and if he looked too closely at it, he had to believe it had begun even before the gunshot wound.

"Now, I have to get going. I don't think Elijah would have tracked me, but the longer I stay here, the more chances there are. I have to get back to the rez."

"You're just going to leave the baby with me?"

Her expression went grim, but it softened when her gaze landed on Mak's sleeping form cradled in Brady's arm. "Unfortunately, I'm a liability to him right now. I have to leave him with someone I can trust."

"They could track your car."

She shook her head. "We walked."

"You...walked. In this rain?"

"I had to. I had to." She cradled her head in her hands again, though she didn't cry, thank God. "I didn't want to tell you this. I didn't want to... It isn't fair, but I can't worry about that when Mak's *life* is in my hands."

She looked up at him—desolate, apologetic. His heart twisted, though he tried to harden himself against that. Against her.

"Elijah idolizes Ace. He worships him. He wants

to *be* him, and not in that Sons way where they'll do whatever Ace did just for power. In a real way. In a real, dangerous way. He wants to take Ace's spot, and he'll do anything to get there."

Brady felt no surprise, no hurt. He should be feeling both of those things, but he couldn't manage it with a soft baby curled up against him. He could only tell her the truth. "I know."

"You know?" Cecilia blinked at Brady, at that harsh, final way he said those two words. "How do you..."

His jaw was set, and that blankness he'd perfected enshrouded his whole being. But his eyes told a different story. There was anguish there. Had she ever seen anguish in Brady?

"I've had run-ins with Elijah for the past eight years," he said, not offering any explanation as to what *run-in* might mean.

"Eight years," Cecilia repeated, just barely keeping the shriek out of her voice, and only for Mak's sake.

"It was happenstance. The first time."

"The first... Brady. What is this?"

"I arrested him. My first arrest actually. When he realized I was a Wyatt...it became something of a game to him. To poke at me. To try and get arrested by me specifically. I assume to prove he could get away with things—and out of jail over and over again. Nothing serious, obviously, but he made it pretty clear he was the next iteration of my father and there was nothing I could do to stop it."

"How come none of you ever told me?"

He turned away from her, Mak still sleeping cradled in his arm like the baby belonged there. "I'm the only one who knows. I didn't think it'd ever touch anyone else."

"Brady." She was utterly speechless. He had a secret from his brothers. She hadn't thought it possible. Oh, there were emotional scars they all kept from each other, anyone who'd grown up in the midst of them knew that. But not actual…secrets.

She'd thought.

"What do you mean—"

"It isn't the point right now. The point is if you really don't want anyone to know you stole this baby—"

"I didn't steal—"

"Then you can't stay. Do you have anything for him? Diapers? Food?"

"Not yet, but there's a plan in place."

"A plan?"

She looked at him for a second, trying to wrap her brain around what was happening. What she was asking, and what he was saying. She'd known Brady would have to go along with some of this because he understood what it was to be a child in the Sons.

But she'd had no idea he had a connection to Elijah. That her life, which had just taken the most complicated turn, would be even more complicated by the man in front of her. She'd always considered him pretty uncomplicated.

"You can't tell me there's something you've never talked to your brothers about, that ties to this child, and then change the subject."

"Except I just did."

"Were you *born* this frustrating or did you have to work really hard at it?"

"Says the woman who brought me a stolen infant."

"He is not stolen," Cecilia replied through gritted teeth. She'd done the right thing, knew that with an absolute certainty that had no room for doubt, and yet he made her feel shame for not finding a legal way to do it. "What would you have done differently, Brady?" she asked, though she was half-afraid he'd have an answer, and a good one.

He looked down at the sleeping baby for the longest time, then finally sighed. "I don't know."

Thank God.

"What's the plan for baby supplies?"

"Felicity and Gage are going to bring you dinner…but it won't be food in the take-out bags."

"And you didn't take the baby to them because…?"

"Felicity has already had her Sons run-in. Besides, she…" Cecilia trailed off. She was usually an expert at keeping secrets, but that one had nearly slipped out.

Brady raised an eyebrow, waiting for her to finish that sentence.

"She has a job. They both do. I know you'd love to

be back at yours, but you can't. Trust me, if I could leave him with Liza or Nina, I would, but I think Elijah would expect that. He's going to look at my sisters harder than he looks into the Wyatts, what with it being my friend's baby and all."

Brady's face was impassive. "He'll look at us too."

"Maybe he will, but I don't trust anyone else." She hated being so baldly honest with him, hated the fact she'd cried in front of him. But she would do it over and over again if it kept Mak safe.

And Mak *looked* safe in Brady's arm. Sleeping against Brady's chest. Brady was too noble not to do everything in his power to keep Mak safe. She had to believe he'd bend some rules for *this*, if nothing else.

"I have to go. Gage and Felicity should be here soon. I'll be in touch." She moved for Brady and Mak. She looked down at the baby she loved and thought about Layla's desperate pleas. All that responsibility weighed heavy.

This small, helpless life was in her hands, and the only way to ensure his safety was to leave him in someone else's.

They were capable hands, though. She looked up at Brady, whose face was way too close for comfort. She'd had a few drinks that night she'd kissed him. Still, she remembered the kiss far more clearly than she remembered the rest of the night. The impulse, the need.

That split second where shock had melted into

response before he'd firmly taken her by the shoulders and pushed her a step back. He'd looked furious.

But there had been that moment. It had scared the life out of her. Just like all the things jangling in her chest right now, looking up at his hazel eyes and knowing he'd take all of what she put on his shoulders.

She stepped back and then turned and headed for the door. She couldn't let herself look back, or even go back to the dryer and get her damp clothes. She had to keep moving forward until Mak was safe. For good.

Chapter Three

Cecilia was right. Felicity and Gage showed up not too long after she left and disappeared into the night. Brady opened the door, keeping the sleeping baby in his arm out of sight.

Gage and his fiancée stood on the threshold. It was still weird. His twin brother and Felicity. Engaged.

It wasn't all that long ago Felicity had had a crush on *him*. Brady had never seen Felicity as more than a little sister. He respected Duke Knight too much to look at any of his foster daughters and see… Whatever it was people saw in each other that made them want to get married, apparently.

Gage had no such qualms. It hadn't taken more than a few months for him to settle into being with Felicity, to propose marriage.

"We brought you dinner," Felicity said, smiling as she held up the bag. They both stepped inside, carefully closing the door behind them.

Without hesitation, Felicity moved across the room to the counter that ran between his kitchen and his living room. She pulled things out of the bags.

"Diapers. Formula. Bottles. We've got some more stuff in a bag in the car. We'll go down and get that later when I leave."

"You mean, when you both leave."

"Nah. I'm bunking," Gage said, settling himself onto the couch easily. "You don't expect to care for an infant on your own, do you?"

"I'm not sure I expect the two of us to do it either."

"We'll figure it out," Gage said, all smiles. Gage liked to lighten a situation with a joke, but this smile was more than just that. It was aimed at Felicity. It was love. "Go on now," he said to her.

"You should," she replied, clasping her hands together.

Gage patted the seat beside him and Felicity went and sat there. They both looked up at him expectantly like he had any idea what they were doing.

"What is with you two?" Brady grumbled.

Gage slung his arm across Felicity's shoulders. "We're going to have a baby," he announced, grinning. Not Gage's typical grin meant to hide everything going on inside his head. No, this was a true smile. True happiness.

Brady blinked. It took a while to realize his brother had not spoken in a foreign language, but had in fact delivered a clear, concise sentence in English. "A baby."

"Real as the one you're holding."

"But... You aren't married yet."

Gage snorted out a laugh and Felicity smiled indulgently.

"Did you need a lesson about the birds and the bees?" Gage asked, with a smirk.

"No. I... A baby. Congratulations."

"I hope you'll be able to say that and mean it at some point," Felicity said gently.

Brady stepped toward them. Irritated with himself for not handling this the right way. "I *am* happy for you. I'm just shocked. It's been a day," he said, looking down at the baby he held. Who wasn't his, but was now his responsibility.

Mak began to squirm, fuss, then cry. Felicity popped off the couch, holding out her arms.

"Can I?"

He handed off the fussing baby and rolled his shoulders, trying not to wince at the pain in his injured one. Felicity rocked and crooned to Mak and Brady looked at his twin brother. They'd shared everything, or close to it. Not everything. Not the separate ways their father had tortured them.

Not Elijah Jones.

"You're going to be a father," Brady offered helplessly.

"Not a word I've ever cared for, but I'll make it mean something different."

"I know you will." It was a strange thing, since Brady wasn't this infant's father, but Gage's news and words crystalized what Brady had to do.

He'd grown up in the Sons. Thanks to his oldest

brother's belief in right and good, Brady had come out believing in right and good, as well. Jamison had sacrificed a lot to get Brady and Gage out of the Sons together. He'd given them the gift of hope, and the gift of each other.

So, Brady believed in laws and rules—the following of them, the enforcing them. Believed in good. In doing the right thing. Always. Because of Jamison's example. Because of Grandma Pauline and the privilege he'd had to escape from the Sons and grow up in a real home, with real love.

But if he truly believed in Jamison's example, it couldn't be just about upholding the law. It had to be about keeping this innocent life out of the Sons. Which meant accepting that he'd bend some rules to do it.

"Gage. I've been keeping a secret," Brady announced.

Gage's eyebrows went up. "What kind?"

"The Sons kind," Brady said grimly.

CECILIA WAS BEING WATCHED. She could feel it, and see the signs of it. Still, she went about her workday. Answering calls. Patrolling the rez. She kept her body on alert, ready to fight off whatever was watching.

But she didn't stop doing what she loved to do. Being a tribal police officer was everything to Cecilia, and even being watched wouldn't stop her from handling her responsibilities.

She didn't remember her early years here with

her mother. Vaguely, in a misty kind of way, she remembered her mother. Mostly, she thought, because
Aunt Eva had made sure of it.

But Aunt Eva had moved Cecilia off the rez and
onto the Knight ranch after Mom had died. Cecilia had been loved, she'd had sisters, and the kind
of stability her mother had never been able to give
her. Aunt Eva had died a few years later, and that
had been hard, but she'd had Duke and her sisters.

Still, she'd missed this feeling of community and
belonging, of having a tie to her history. Maybe she
spent an awful lot of time seeing the bad parts of the
rez as a police officer, but she'd needed to figure herself out as an adult there. Right there.

She liked to think she had figured herself out,
but this situation with Layla and Mak was testing
everything she'd learned since joining the tribal police seven years ago.

No doubt she was being watched because Elijah
knew she'd taken Mak. Which meant there was no
hope of sneaking off to Brady's tonight and visit-
ing him.

She'd be able to call, though. Elijah wouldn't be
able to intercept that. So, she'd call and make sure
Mak was okay and it would have to be enough for
now.

It didn't feel okay. She'd left that sweet little boy
with a stranger, and no matter how she knew that
stranger was one of the best men on earth, Mak didn't.

Cecilia walked down the road toward her house.

She waved at her elderly neighbor who liked to tell her stories about her mother. Cecilia wasn't sure they were true, but she liked listening to them nonetheless.

But when she saw her front door open behind the screen door, Cecilia didn't have time for neighborly chats. She hurried inside through the screen door, heart pounding in panic, hand on the butt of her weapon.

But it was no intruder. Cecilia's hands fell to her sides. "Rach?"

Rachel was in the kitchen, puttering around with making tea. She flashed a smile. "Hi. You're home early."

"What are you doing here?" It wasn't unusual for her cousin to visit, or to spend nights with her. Rachel was a teacher on the rez, and she split her time between here and the Knight ranch so she could keep an eye on her father when she wasn't teaching.

Normally, Cecilia loved having Rachel underfoot. She liked having company in this house. She loved her cousin, who'd been like a sister growing up.

But Rachel had been visually impaired since she was a toddler. Normally Cecilia didn't even think of it. Rachel knew how to get around. She'd dealt with the impairment since she was a child, and now she was an adult who could take care of herself.

Today, with someone watching Cecilia's every step, the last thing she wanted was Rachel here. She'd be vulnerable to whatever Cecilia had gotten herself wrapped up in, and more so because she wouldn't necessarily see an attack coming.

"Rach. I..." Rachel was Aunt Eva and Uncle Duke's only biological daughter. In some ways, Rachel and Cecilia had a closer connection because of that biology—cousins. Not because they didn't think of Eva and Duke's foster daughters as their sisters, but because the foster girls had always felt a certain kind of jealousy toward the biological relations.

It had never impacted their friendship, their love for one another. Cecilia would lay down her life for any of them, just as she knew they'd do the same for her. The four other Knight girls were her *sisters*. Luckily adulthood had smoothed over a lot if not all of those old resentments, but it didn't erase the special bond she had with Rachel.

Rachel was like her baby sister. She wanted to protect her. "You shouldn't be here today."

"Why not?"

Cecilia couldn't tell Rachel, no matter how much she wanted to. She'd already involved Gage, Felicity and Brady. Adding more people would be dangerous. For them.

The Wyatts and Knights had been through enough danger in the past few months.

And every time a Knight goes to a Wyatt man for help—what happens?

She shook that thought away. Liza had asked for Jamison's help, yes, and they were getting married and raising Liza's half sister. But they'd been together as teenagers.

Which was the same as Cody and Nina, who'd already eloped and were living in Bonesteel with their daughter after a teenage romance that had been broken up by the Sons, then rekindled again.

As for Felicity and Gage, well, that was a bit of a shock, and an odd pairing, but they made each other happy.

It was a parade of coincidences that had nothing to do with Cecilia and Brady.

"Cee, what's going on?" Rachel asked.

Cecilia forced herself to smile. "It's been a rough day." Rachel was already here, so sending her away wouldn't do any good.

"And you were hoping to be alone?"

"Yes. No. It's fine." Rachel was here. Whoever was watching Cecilia had seen her be dropped off and come inside. Cecilia just had to figure out a way to mitigate the situation.

She wanted to go to her room and cry. Or better yet, go home to the Knight ranch and hide from all of this.

But she wasn't weak—couldn't be, for Layla as much as for herself. She hadn't become a police officer because it was easy. She didn't want to help people only when it was comfortable.

Still, this was the biggest challenge of her career, of her *life*. Which meant doubts and fears and wanting to cry was normal. She just couldn't give in to those things. And she couldn't let on to Rachel that she felt them.

"You going to cook me dinner?" Cecilia asked, trying to infuse some levity into her tone.

"That's my lot in life," Rachel returned. "Cooking for a passel of helpless Knights."

"Helpless seems harsh. And not a word Sarah would appreciate." Sarah was the only one of the Knight girls who'd taken an interest in ranching, keeping her at home full-time. She was everything a ranching woman should be—tough, hardworking, and hardheaded.

"But it fits when she refuses to even learn how to make spaghetti. I won't be around forever."

A blip of panic bloomed in Cecilia's chest, but she kept her tone light. "Going somewhere?"

Rachel shrugged restlessly. "You got off the ranch. You have a life."

"You do too. You're here every summer and—"

"And driven by my daddy. Or my sister, which is fine. The rez isn't for me like it is for you. But maybe the ranch isn't either. Felicity is getting married and having a baby and I… Well, I'm never going to meet anyone the way my life currently is."

"Just get yourself into a life-threatening situation like Felicity did. Brady will follow in Gage's footsteps of falling for the damsel in distress and *bang*."

Rachel wrinkled her nose. "Felicity was hardly a damsel. Besides, Brady is so…stuffy."

"He's not—" Cecilia clamped her mouth shut. Defending Brady's stuffiness was not what she needed to be doing right now. Luckily, a knock on the door made the subject easy to change. It was probably Mrs. Eldridge wanting to share another story. "Be right back," Cecilia said, heading for the front door.

She opened it, expecting her elderly neighbor's face and finding no one. She looked around. No kids giggling in the bushes playing ding-dong-ditch. Just…quiet.

She began to close the door before she noticed the small lump of fur on the porch. Cecilia stopped short as her stomach heaved.

There was an arrow sticking out of it, though the prairie dog clearly hadn't been killed by an arrow. Cecilia swallowed, forced herself to look, to pay attention.

Worse than the fact it was a tiny dead prairie dog, there was a note attached to the arrow with three simple words written on it in capital letters.

See you soon.

She stared at the scrawled words until her vision blurred. She was only shaken out of her frozen state by Rachel's voice.

"Who is it?" Rachel called.

"Just a prank," Cecilia replied, swallowing down the bile in her throat as her fingers closed over the butt of her holstered gun. "I'll be right back." She stepped outside, closing the door behind her. She scanned the area—houses, a quiet street, no one skulking around.

Anymore.

She let her hand fall off her weapon. She'd dispose of the dead animal, and then get Rachel the hell back to the Knight ranch.

Then she'd play Elijah's game, she decided grimly. It was the only way to keep him off Mak's trail.

Chapter Four

Brady was bleary-eyed the next day. Since Mak had slept so much before Felicity had left, he'd spent most of the night up and fussy. Brady and Gage had a list of instructions on baby care, but it had still taken three tries and watching a how-to video online to get the diaper on right. Making bottles and feeding them to the kid was pretty easy, and Mak was mostly a happy baby. Still, Brady was glad Gage was here with him. He wouldn't have survived the night without help—at least not with his sanity intact.

Brady had filled Gage in about Elijah...to an extent. There were things he hadn't told his brothers. The reasons he'd had for keeping Elijah a secret still existed, so keeping some parts of his story to himself made sense. Giving them the truth didn't mean giving them *all* the truths.

It bothered him that he hadn't heard from Cecilia. Not even a text. Shouldn't she want to check in on the baby? What was he supposed to do all day? Gage would go in to work, and Brady couldn't keep having visitors. If someone was watching or looking into him, the trail of people would be suspect.

Not as suspect as it might be at another time in his life. People had been traipsing in and out of his apartment to help out for too long now. Maybe it wouldn't send up any red flags, but there was no reason to chance it.

Gage had smuggled up a foldable, portable crib thing in his duffel bag. Mak was currently sleeping peacefully, and Brady knew he should try to catch a few hours too. Maybe even wake the baby up in an effort to keep him on a correct day/night schedule.

But he couldn't bring himself to wake up the boy when he looked so peaceful, and Brady's shoulder was currently throbbing too much to sleep through.

He went to the kitchen and made coffee, took some ibuprofen and the last of his antibiotics—praying they worked this time. He was tired of hospitals and doctors and being poked at and *hmm*ed over.

Gage came out of the spare bedroom dressed in his uniform. It was the last week he'd be putting that particular uniform on. He was transferring from Valiant County to Rapid City PD to be closer to Felicity's job at the National Park, and Brady still hadn't fully grasped the reality of not working with his twin brother anymore.

"I know you miss it," Gage said, either not understanding the pain Brady felt, or purposefully changing the topic to another painful one.

Brady gestured at his bum shoulder, tried to sound nonchalant. "Not much I can do with this."

"It's not permanent."

"No." It felt it, though. He was *supposed* to be back at work by now, not sidelined by an infection. He was *supposed* to go back to work knowing Gage would be there, but Gage only had three shifts left before his life changed.

He'd marry Felicity, have a kid, be a cop somewhere else.

If Brady looked too closely at all that, he might find the source of the low feelings he'd been having before he'd been shot.

So he decided not to look closely. "Coffee?"

"I'll just grab some at the station. I want to check on Felicity before my shift starts. She's feeling a little off in the mornings."

"It fits, you know, you two. I wouldn't have predicted it. But it works." Brady didn't know what possessed him to say it, but there it was.

Gage grinned. "Yeah, I know." His smile dimmed. "This Elijah…" Gage sighed. "What do I tell the others?"

Brady loved all of his brothers—would fight next to, protect and die for every single one of them. But he and Gage had escaped the Sons together, thanks to Jamison. They'd been together from the very beginning, and no matter how old they got, there was a deeper bond or connection between them. They were twins.

The fact Gage was willing to keep part of the story a secret from their brothers only made Brady feel guilty that there were still things Gage didn't know.

Brady didn't like to deal in guilt—he refused to wallow in it. If a man was guilty, he needed to change his actions to not feel guilty anymore. Maybe there'd been reasons to keep Elijah a secret, but the reasons had lost their weight.

"I think I should tell them. Everything. Together. I don't think Mak and I should stay here. I think we should hide. I just have to figure out how I can get him somewhere without being seen—and making sure Cecilia is okay."

"Heard from her?"

Brady shook his head.

"I don't like it. I know she can take care of herself, but I don't like it."

"Same, but I also know there's no getting through to that hardheaded woman." Brady didn't know why she had to be contrary for the sake of being contrary, but he knew she would be. No matter what he said.

"Let's set up a family dinner. Cecilia comes and you come. We find a way to hide Mak. If everyone descends on the ranch and there's no baby—it'll throw anyone off the sent."

"But how do we completely hide the presence of a six-month-old?"

Brady looked down at the baby in the portable crib. Mak was still fast asleep, little fist bunched and tucked under his chin, knees bent but spread wide-open. Felicity had brought some clothes so he was wearing dinosaur footie pajamas.

Though he didn't say anything, Brady could tell Gage was thinking about his future as a father.

"I hate to bring anyone else into it…"

Gage fixed him with a stern look. "I think you know everyone else would be more than happy to help keep that or any child out of the Sons' clutches."

Brady nodded. He knew it was true, but it was still against that moral compass he'd always listened to. Don't bring more people than necessary into Sons danger. Especially innocent ones.

"Gigi has that doll she carries around. She was even pushing it around in a stroller last time she was at the ranch." Brady shrugged away the guilt that was already poking at him. Gigi was four, and though she'd spent most of those four years in the Sons' camps before Liza and Jamison had saved her, she didn't deserve to be dragged back into it.

"Mak's a bit bigger than a doll, but it's not the worst plan," Gage said thoughtfully. "Especially if it's just between apartment door and truck. I bet Cody could find us a truck with tinted windows." Gage rubbed a hand over his jaw. "I'll make the arrangements."

"I can—"

"You got a baby to take care of. You take care of him. I'll take care of getting him to the ranch."

Brady looked at Mak's sleeping form. Completely

and utterly defenseless. Brady might want to protect him all on his own, but this child deserved everyone he had in his arsenal.

"Let's do it as soon as possible."

THE NICE THING about Rachel staying with her was that Cecilia was so worried about Rachel, she didn't have much worry left for herself. She spent a sleepless night checking and rechecking the doors and windows in her house to make sure they were locked.

Bleary-eyed the next morning, she subsisted off coffee—which she normally didn't drink—and as much sugar as one human could possibly stand. She did a quick walk around the house looking for any more dead animals or threatening notes.

As she stepped back inside, Rachel was shuffling into the kitchen with a big, loud yawn. Rach had never been a morning person. Cecilia didn't know why she'd taken a teaching job that required her to do most of her work in the morning, but she could only assume Rachel loved it.

When Rachel stayed with her, she usually walked to and from the school with her probing cane. Cecilia would feel better if she had a support dog, but Rachel had lost hers last year to old age and hadn't had the heart to go through the process of trying to get a new one.

"I'm going to drive you in today."

Rachel frowned as she deftly poured herself some coffee. "Why would you do that?"

Cecilia had prepared for that question, and still she winced. She hated to lie to Rachel. So she didn't lie…exactly. "There's been some stuff going on. Pranks most likely, but the kind that can escalate if given the opportunity."

Rachel's frown deepened. "That's vague."

"It's a vague kind of thing. You'd probably be fine walking, but it'd make me feel better if I drove you."

Rachel sighed a little, and Cecilia half expected her to press the matter.

"It's too early to argue," she said around another yawn. "But I'm walking back after my classes are done."

Cecilia tried not to snap that it wasn't an option. Compromise was the best bet when talking to a stubborn Knight woman—she should know. "Can you walk with someone? Maybe one of your older students?"

"If you really think it's necessary."

"I do."

Rachel shrugged and sipped her coffee. "I'll be ready in about twenty."

While she waited, Cecilia rechecked the house to make sure it was all locked up. She called in on her radio to start her shift, and drove Rachel to the school.

The morning was warm but with a hint of a chill. Fall was starting its slow unfurling, usually Cecilia's favorite time of year.

It wouldn't be this year with Layla in the hospital and trying to keep Mak from Elijah and the state.

Cecilia pulled to a stop in front of the school, tried to bite her tongue and failed. "Don't forget to have someone walk with you back to the house. Someone you trust," she said as Rachel got out of the car.

Rachel paused. "You're going to have to tell me what this is all about."

"When I've got more information, I will," Cecilia lied.

Rachel made a disbelieving sound, then closed the car door and walked toward the school. Cecilia watched until she disappeared inside.

Once she was sure Rachel was inside, she did her normal rounds. It didn't appear she was being followed today, which was only a minor relief. Someone could start at any moment.

After her first call of the day, a minor vandalism situation that had been solved by involving the mother of the teenage perpetrator, she almost felt relaxed.

Of course, that was when she noticed her tail. She tried to act nonchalant, to keep doing her job, but every hour it was harder to pretend to be unaffected. If they were watching her, was Rachel safe? If they were following *her*, would Rachel be left alone?

If they were following her in particular, what would they do if they found her isolated and alone?

Nothing, because you're a trained police officer carrying many weapons with which to defend yourself.

She wanted to believe that voice in her head, to feel sure of it, but she also knew she was *one* police officer. She didn't know how many people were following her.

She got another call, this time a disturbance, and had to put her stalkers out of her mind while she tried to make peace between two neighbors fighting about property lines. It was an annoying, pointless screaming match—but it was her job to smooth it over.

It took a full hour, and her head pounded by the time she was walking back to her patrol car. People who couldn't—wouldn't—compromise always gave her a headache.

She glanced at her watch. Rachel would have walked to the house by now. Maybe Cecilia could drive by the house, just check in on her. Pretend like she'd forgotten her lunch and was grabbing a sandwich so Rachel didn't get unduly worried.

The pounding in her head stopped, as did her breath and perhaps even her heart when she saw a piece of paper tucked under her windshield wiper. It fluttered in the breeze.

It could be anything, but Cecilia knew what it would be. Another note—sans dead animal this time.

Or so she thought, until she stepped closer to her patrol car. Under the wheel was a dead raccoon. As if she'd run it over.

But she hadn't.

No, it was another sign. Another warning.

Steeling herself for another threatening note, Cecilia pulled a rubber glove out of the glove pouch on her gun belt. She picked up the note and read it.

She's pretty.

Cecilia didn't let herself react outwardly. Inside she was ice, her heart a shivering mass of fear and panic. But outside, her hands were steady and her gaze was cool. She slid into the patrol car and set the note carefully on the passenger seat, pulling off the glove as she did so.

She turned the ignition, calmly eased on the gas. Keeping her attention evenly split between phone and road, she clicked Rachel's name on her phone screen and called.

The phone rang. And rang.

"Pick up," Cecilia muttered, swearing when it went to voice mail.

She was tempted to increase her speed, fly through the rez to her house on the eastern edge.

The only *she* the note could refer to was Rachel. It was a threat against Rachel, and Rachel was alone. Cecilia should have predicted this. Should have insisted Rachel…

What? Not teach her class? Hide away? It wouldn't have been a fair demand, but Cecilia still knew she should have done *something*.

Cecilia drove within the speed limit, watching her surroundings in case it was a trap. An ambush. Because threatening Rachel was only about getting to her. Rachel didn't know anything.

Or would Elijah think she did?

Cecilia swore again, increasing her speed, though not enough to draw attention. She came to a screeching halt in front of her house. If anyone was watching or following, she'd broken her calm facade.

Since she already had, she raced inside, hand on the butt of her weapon. But Rachel was safe as could be, curled up on the couch, earbuds in.

She pulled one out and looked at Cecilia's form with raised eyebrows. "Everything okay?"

Cecilia let out a ragged breath. This couldn't go on. She knew Elijah was purposefully trying to scare her, and giving in to threats and scare tactics would give him what he wanted, but...

She couldn't risk Rachel.

"I have to take you back to the ranch."

"Cee, you're being super weird this week." Rachel's expression wasn't confused so much as concerned. "You're going to have to tell me what's going on."

"I know. I know. Look... I'll explain everything when we're home. With everyone." She had to fill everyone in on what was happening. It was the only way to keep Rachel and Mak safe. To make sure none of them were brought unwittingly into this.

Because Elijah was clearly ready and willing to threaten everything she loved. She didn't have to live with threats. She should act.

"Let's get to the ranch," Cecilia said. "I just have to call someone to take the last two hours of my shift."

"I can have Dad—"

"No. No, I'm taking you."

"This is really bad, isn't it?" Rachel asked, twisting her fingers together.

Cecilia didn't mind lying to the people she loved if it saved them from worry, but she wasn't sure she had that luxury anymore. "It could be, if I'm not very careful."

Rachel slid off the couch, crossed the room and took Cecilia's hands in hers and gave them a squeeze. "Then let's be very, very careful."

Chapter Five

Brady had faced unhinged people with guns, big men so high on drugs nothing short of severe use of force would subdue them, and a slew of other scary, life-threatening situations in his tenure as a police officer and EMT.

He had been shot trying to save Felicity from her father, had hiked the Badlands trying to find his brother before Ace killed him. At eleven, he and Gage had almost been caught escaping the Sons.

Yet none of those instances had ever made him as bone-deep *afraid* as the one he found himself in right now. Even in the moment he and Gage had been found by a member of the Sons. Brady had been sure they'd be dead, but instead the man had let them go.

He'd been murdered days later.

Why this was more terrifying, Brady had no idea. Liza was buckling Mak into the doll stroller Gigi had happily pushed into his apartment. Gigi was now holding the doll, making funny faces at Mak in an effort to make him laugh.

Brady couldn't say he'd been particularly welcoming when Liza had shown back up in their lives a few months ago. As the oldest brother, Jamison had gotten all of them out of the Sons before he'd saved himself. When he'd saved himself, he'd brought Liza with him. The Knights had taken her in and Brady had always assumed Jamison and Liza would live happily-ever-after.

He'd had to believe it was possible. Then Liza had left, gone back to the Sons, breaking Jamison's heart. Brady had never let on how much that had affected him. He secretly wondered if they weren't a little cursed by the Wyatt name.

It hadn't helped when Cody's girlfriend Nina, another Knight foster, had also taken off. Not to the Sons but to no one knew where.

A few months ago, Liza had reappeared, needing Jamison's help to save Gigi, her half sister, from the Sons. A while after that, Nina had shown up, gunshot wound and all, needing Cody's help to keep their daughter safe.

And somehow, they were all back together and happy with it. Like the time in between didn't matter.

As an adult, Brady didn't know what to make of it. How to reconcile the things he'd begun to think were impossible, with what was in front of him. Possible and growing.

"It'll be fine," Liza reassured him, likely misreading the course of his thoughts. "Gigi will be gentle."

Brady had no doubt Gigi would handle this with the utmost care. Even at four, she'd dealt with more than most kids should ever handle. "He could make a noise."

"He could," Liza agreed, crouching to give Mak's belly a tickle. The baby gurgled appreciatively. "But Gigi and I will be chatting loud enough to cover any baby sounds."

Brady looked dubiously at Mak. He'd heard the boy scream pretty effectively for all manner of reasons, but he was freshly fed, changed, napped and seemed happy enough.

"I didn't want to drag you and Gigi into this."

Liza stood slowly, and she fixed Brady with a look. "I don't know why it's so hard for you hard-headed Wyatts to realize we were there too. Even Gigi knows what it's like in there. We'd always be part of helping someone stay far away from the Sons. No matter the risk. Because it's always worth the risk to get out."

Brady looked down at Gigi, who looked up at him solemnly. She was wearing a pink T-shirt that said *Girl Power* in sequins.

She knew too much for a girl of almost five. Brady knew, from his own experience, that escaping at eleven had given him a determination to *help*. And even as young as Gigi was, he saw that in her expression.

"All right. Let's go."

GIGI WAS GIVEN the stroller. Liza pulled the hood down so that it obscured all but Mak's feet.

Gigi took her job as pusher very seriously, slowly and carefully pushing it forward. Mak babbled in baby talk, but Liza started talking over it. She asked Gigi about some TV show Gigi liked and Gigi began a monologue on the merits of each character.

God bless her.

He and Liza worked to carry the stroller down the stairs, Gigi admonishing them to be careful with her baby.

They reached the tinted truck they'd borrowed for the occasion. Brady tried to search the perimeter without giving away that's what he was doing. He didn't spot anyone, but that didn't mean they weren't being watched.

"Now, you go on and get in your car seat," Liza said to Gigi, helping her into the back seat.

"Make sure you buckle my baby in," Gigi ordered sternly. She was an excellent actress, though she did give Brady a little wink as she scrambled across the back seat.

Liza sighed as if it were a silly request. "Dolls can't get hurt, sissy. It's a little silly to—"

"You *have* to buckle her in. Just like me," Gigi insisted.

Liza rolled her eyes and nodded and bent down to pick up Mak. He made a little squealing sound, but Liza had angled her body so that it would be almost impossible for any watcher to see what was supposed to be a doll actually wiggle.

Gigi started singing the ABCs at full volume, clearly obscuring Mak's noises.

Brady could only watch in awe as these two people managed to enact his plan even better than he'd imagined, and without a hitch.

"Hop in the passenger seat, cowboy," Liza said as she closed the back door.

"I can drive."

"No, you can't."

Brady scowled at Liza. "I've been cleared to drive." His shoulder was feeling moderately better. He hadn't even wanted to cut it off when he woke up this morning. It was possible the last round of antibiotics had worked.

Liza snorted. "My truck. I drive. Those are the rules, bud. Now, you can stay here, or you can come out to the ranch for some of Grandma Pauline's potato casserole."

She was still playacting, and continuing the argument would make it seem more important than it was. So he had to suck up his control issues and go to the passenger side.

If he grumbled to himself a little bit while he did it, no one had to know. He slid into the seat and closed the door and then let out a long breath. They'd gotten through one hard part successfully, he thought. Mostly because of the precocious little girl in the back seat.

Brady twisted in his seat, though it hurt his shoulder, and gave Gigi a big grin. "Gigi, you're a star."

She beamed at him. "I like pretending. And I like Mak. We're going to keep him away from the bad men."

"Yes, we are." He turned back to face forward. From inside the truck he could do a better scan. Still no one. He blew out a breath, warning himself not to relax. There was a lot that could go wrong yet.

But one hurdle had been jumped.

Gigi entertained Mak in the back seat by talking and making faces. Mak happily gurgled and drooled back. Brady let himself watch that, reminding himself that he wasn't so much bringing Liza and Gigi into danger as letting them help an innocent child escape it.

They'd both crossed Ace, in a way, and so they were already living under that specter—no matter how many high-security prisons the man was put in.

Brady scanned the highway in front of them, then glanced in the rearview mirror. There was a lone Chevy truck. Something about it didn't sit right with Brady.

"Speed up," he ordered.

Liza raised an eyebrow, not taking her eyes off the road. "Tone, Brady."

Brady didn't have the patience to sweet-talk Liza. "Not crazy speed. Just enough so I can tell if this Chevy is pacing us."

This time she didn't make a snarky comment, she did as he asked. When the Chevy kept pace, Brady inwardly swore. He kept that emotion out of his voice when he spoke. "We have a tail."

"That doesn't mean he knows we have Mak," Liza said calmly, reaching across the console and resting her hand on his arm. "In fact, if we can convince him we *don't*, all the better."

Brady flicked a glance at Mak in the car seat. Gigi had reached across the space between their car seats and was holding his squirming baby hand in hers.

"Then I guess that's what we have to do."

CECILIA DROVE OFF the reservation, watching her rear-view mirror. She hadn't spotted a tail yet, but that didn't mean there wouldn't be one. Surely Elijah or his "buddies" hadn't simply stopped following Liza because she'd left the rez.

But she made it miles and miles down the mostly empty highway. If she saw a car, it usually passed her or was headed in the opposite direction. Cecilia knew she should relax as mile by mile they continued without being followed.

But she couldn't seem to let her guard down. Elijah wouldn't give up that easily, which meant he had something else up his sleeve.

If they made it home, she'd have help. Support. She didn't want to bring her family into this, but her family was already in danger. She might have felt guilty for getting involved in the first place, but all she could think of was Layla lost in the dark cloud that had become her life.

She'd begged for help. Begged for a chance to be a mother to her child.

There was no way Cecilia could have turned away from that, even to protect her family. And she knew, because of how her family was made up, because of what they'd been through, there was no way her family would have wanted her to turn away from Layla.

They'd *want* to be part of the fight too. So many of them had been impacted by the Sons. The Knights were not the kind to turn away from the dangerous just to save their own skin. The Wyatts even less so.

Thinking of it made Cecilia feel a little teary, so she focused on the road. On getting home.

When they weren't too far away from the turn off the highway to head toward home, both her and Rachel's phones chimed in unison.

Rachel sighed as she dug her phone out of her purse. "I really hate simultaneous texts. They're never good." She hit the button for her phone to read her text to her.

From: Gage Wyatt
Knight-Wyatt dinner at Grandma Pauline's. Everyone mandatory.

"Do they have to be so bossy?" Cecilia muttered. Then she frowned. "Brady can't go." How was he going to get out of "everyone mandatory"? Or would he try to bring Mak to the ranch? Surely not.

"Why can't Brady go and why do you know that?"

Cecilia didn't want to explain the whole thing yet. She only wanted to go through it once, hear all the disapproval once. And there was going to be some *serious* disapproval. "We'll get to that. Just text him that we're already on our way."

Rachel used her voice-to-text to send the reply.

Cecilia signaled the turn onto the gravel road that would lead them to the Reaves Ranch, Grandma Pauline's spread.

Instead of making an easy turn, Cecilia heard a faint pop, then the car rumbled and the steering wheel jerked. Cecilia almost lost her grip, but managed to tighten her hold at the last second. She braked a little too hard, fishtailing and tipping precariously into the gravel.

She managed to wrestle the truck to a stop, and quickly braked. She wasn't sure what had happened, but that pop she'd heard had sounded like a gunshot to her.

"Stay put," Cecilia ordered, heart hammering in her chest. Still, her voice was calm and authoritative.

She slid out of the driver's side, pulling the gun out of its holster but holding it behind her as she eyed the area. A big truck slowed to a stop on the highway a few yards away from where she stood.

She kept the gun out of sight as the driver leaned out of the window. "Need some help?" The man offered a pleasant enough smile. Cecilia was also certain she'd seen this same exact man come out of Layla's house with Elijah. It had been a long time ago, probably a year or two, but Cecilia rarely forgot a face. Especially one that ugly.

She fixed a grateful smile on her lips. "Oh, wow.

That would be so great! I've got a spare in the back, but changing a tire can be such a pain."

The man smirked and shoved his truck into Park. It looked like there was potentially another passenger in the vehicle, but hiding. Cecilia pretended like she didn't notice. He slid out of the truck and there was a gun in his hand as a sleazy grin spread across his face.

Cecilia didn't pause, didn't hesitate. She kicked straight out, landing the blow on the gun itself and knocking it out of the man's hands. She pivoted quickly, landing an elbow against his jaw. A nasty cracking sound whipped through the air and blood spattered.

Cecilia didn't have time to wince, she had to duck the returning blow. She didn't duck low enough and it clipped her head. Which probably hurt his hand more than her skull, all in all. But the satisfaction of missing most of that blow knocked her off-balance for the next, which hit her right in the cheekbone.

Pain flashed behind her eyes, but she could hear someone approaching. She didn't have time to even suck in a breath. She landed a knee to the man's groin and he let out a wheezing breath as he fumbled. She whirled to face the man, gun at the ready.

He had his own, so she shot, aiming for the arm so he'd drop the gun, ideally before getting off his own shot. She wanted both of them alive. They might have useful information after all, but if either of them went for Rachel, she'd shoot to kill.

The man howled and dropped his gun as the bullet hit him in the forearm. Blood gushed and he grabbed his arm and screamed.

The other man was crawling toward the dropped gun, still wheezing, but Cecilia quickly scooped it up off the ground. She held one gun on each man and eyed them with disgust.

"Elijah sent you."

"He'll keep sending more," the man she'd cracked in the jaw replied with a bloody smile.

"And I'll keep kicking their asses," Cecilia replied with a shrug. "Rach?"

"I already called Gage," Rachel said. Apparently she'd gotten out of the truck during the fight, but Cecilia had been concentrating too hard on the men to notice. "He's not on duty, but he called dispatch for us."

The faint sound of sirens wailed in the distance, a sign that help was on its way. "Guess you boys are headed to jail," Cecilia said with a smile. "Anything you want to tell me about your buddy?"

The one she'd shot had stopped screaming, but he looked at her with cold eyes as he gripped his bleeding arm. "He's going to get you. He's going to make you pay. He'll only kill you if you're lucky."

A cold shiver went through Cecilia, but she didn't let it show outwardly. "He's going to try all those things, and he's going to fail. Just like you."

She tried to believe her own words, but the cold chill remained as she waited for backup.

Chapter Six

Brady paced the living room at Grandma Pauline's, Mak snuggled into his good arm. The boy cried if he tried to put him anywhere else or give him to anyone else. As it was, he wasn't sleeping. He was simply looking up at Brady with big brown eyes, a serious expression on his little face.

Brady didn't know what to do with *that*, or Gage currently coordinating officers to arrest the men who'd attacked Cecilia.

Brady didn't know if it was the same men who'd tailed him and Liza yet, but his tail hadn't approached them. They'd kept driving when Liza had turned off onto the gravel road to Grandma Pauline's.

Gage strode into the room, and Brady didn't even let him speak before he was peppering him with questions.

"Make and model?"

Gage's expression was grave. "Same as yours. They must have backtracked and waited for Cecilia and Rach."

Brady swore.

"It might not be such a bad thing."

At Brady's glare, Gage held up his hands. "You— the guy with the baby they're looking for—were deemed not as important. That means they don't know where Mak is."

"I don't think Cecilia and Rach being a target is a *good* thing."

"I didn't say that. I said it's not such a *bad thing*, because it means they don't know where the baby is. Based on the condition of the two men that tried to ambush Cecilia, I don't think we need to worry too much about her safety."

Brady grunted. He knew Cecilia could take care of herself. She was a fine cop, even if he didn't always agree with her methods. But it only took one second to be taken down. Since he was currently the one with a gunshot wound that wouldn't heal, he thought he had some perspective on the matter.

But it wouldn't do to argue with Gage over it.

"You want me to take him for a bit?"

Brady gave a shrug. "Seems to be happy here. Where are Cecilia and Rachel?"

"Should be any minute. Just finishing up giving their statements." As if on cue, they heard a commotion in the kitchen. Both men moved toward it.

Mak began to squirm in Brady's arms as he registered Cecilia's voice. Still, Brady stopped cold when he saw her.

Grandma Pauline was bustling around her while Duke Knight demanded to know what was going on. Sarah and Liza helped Grandma gather ice and towels, Tuck led Rachel to the table where Dev was already sitting with Felicity. Wyatt boys and Knight girls—men and women now—always working together to help each other.

"Well. Have that seat, right there." Grandma Pauline motioned to Cecilia, pulling an empty chair out from the table.

"I'm fine," Cecilia said, but she was already moving for the chair because God knew you didn't argue with Grandma Pauline.

Her eye was swollen. Blood was spattered across her shirt, but it didn't look like it was hers. When Gage had told him there'd been an incident, but Cecilia had taken care of it, Brady didn't realize "incident" meant fight and "taken care of it" meant gotten hurt in the process.

Something dark and vicious twisted inside of him. Brady couldn't say he fully understood it. He'd felt similar when seeing what his father or the Sons had done to his brothers—but this had a sharper edge to it. Not just anger. Not just revenge. Something closer to vengeance than he'd ever felt.

"You hand that baby over now," Grandma Pauline ordered Brady, already settling a bag of frozen peas over Cecilia's eye. "Nothing better for a few bumps and bruises than holding a sweet little boy."

It took everyone in the kitchen turning to stare at him to be able to move, to relax some of the fury on his face. To just…breathe. He met Cecilia's confused gaze past the bag of peas Grandma Pauline held under her one eye.

He had a flash of that ill-fated New Year's Eve kiss. Where she'd been laughing at him, poking at him. She'd kissed him out of some kind of…dare inside of herself, he'd always been sure.

But something had changed when she'd pressed her lips to his. A seismic shift inside him. An opening up of something he'd wanted closed. Maybe *that* was the moment everything had started to unravel for him.

It was all her fault, he was sure of that. If only he could be sure of what was winding through him, tying him into knots.

Mak squirmed, started babbling somewhat intensely, breaking Brady from the moment. He looked down at the baby, then remembered what Grandma Pauline had told him to do. He moved to Cecilia's chair and had to kneel down so he could shift Mak into Cecilia's waiting arms. It required getting close, smelling her shampoo, brushing her arm.

Cecilia still looked at him, as if she could see into his thoughts. As if it shook her as deeply as it shook him.

He stepped away, shoved his hands into his pockets. He was losing it. Hallucinating due to lack of sleep. That was all.

That was *all*.

"I guess some of you need an introduction," Cecilia said softly, looking down at Mak. She took a deep breath, gazing down at him. "I had wanted to wait for…"

The door open and Jamison walked in with Cody and Nina and their daughter, Brianna.

"…the Bonesteel contingent," Cecilia finished.

If Brady wasn't totally mistaken, she seemed a little deflated everyone had shown up so quickly. But there was no more putting it off.

"You explain your end, then I'll explain mine," Brady said. Maybe it came out more like an order, but he wasn't feeling particularly genial or accommodating at the moment.

"Yours?" Cecilia asked, just enough acid in her tone to get his back up.

Brady'd kept one secret from his family, from Gage in particular, in his entire life. And it was this. Everything culminating with Cecilia needing his help.

Would he have ever told if she hadn't? If her problem hadn't connected to Elijah through this innocent child?

Would-haves didn't matter, because this—what was in front of him—was all he had. "Yes, my thing. My connection to Elijah, and why I think we need to disappear."

THE ENTIRE KITCHEN seemed to go supersonic. A cacophony of noises and arguments on top of arguments. Cecilia winced against the noise, then against the pain in her cheek.

Cecilia wouldn't admit it out loud, but a few of the jerk's blows had landed and left her feeling sore and achy. At least she'd taken the two guys out all on her own.

She had to admit, Grandma Pauline was close to being right. Mak in her arms didn't take away the pain, but it certainly shifted the pain to something bearable under a curtain of calm.

Mak was safe. No matter what happened today, no matter what would happen after today, Mak was safe. Maybe she should have brought him to both families in the first place, but she wouldn't beat herself up for what could have been.

He was here now, a large group of people ready and willing to fight for him.

Tucker had said, from his standpoint as detective, he thought the men she'd beaten up had followed Brady and Liza first. They'd given up on them and switched their gears for Cecilia and Rachel.

Which meant they didn't know Mak had been in the car with Brady the whole time.

She couldn't relax completely of course. Elijah would keep coming for her, and she was *here* now, which meant he or his men would be soon enough. But Cody had all sorts of security on the Reaves Ranch.

This was the safest place.

And Brady wanted to disappear? No way.

A piercing whistle stopped the competing voices. Grandma Pauline scowled at all of them. "Now. How are we ever going to know what to be mad about if we don't let them explain themselves? Boy—"

"Cecilia needs to go first," Brady said.

Usually it amused Cecilia that Grandma Pauline still called any of the Wyatt brothers *boys*, when they hadn't been that for a very long time. Even more amused that they answered to it without complaint.

But Cecilia couldn't find the means to be amused right now. Mak was in her lap, happily squirming and talking to her in his own language. His dark eyes were wide, trusting.

And she knew without a shadow of a doubt she'd have to leave him again.

But first she had to explain Mak and her dilemma to all the Wyatts and all the Knights. *Then* she'd have to figure out how to disappear…and lead Elijah away.

Which was going to be quite the challenge with *all* these voices in her ears.

"Let's start with the simple question," Grandma Pauline said. "Who's the boy?"

Cecilia explained who Mak was, and how she'd taken him to Brady because she thought he'd be protected there. "He was protected too. Elijah knows I took him, but he hasn't figured out where. So, that's our priority. Keep Mak a secret."

"We're all here. How much of a secret could it be?" Brady demanded.

There was a dark, edgy look in his demeanor that was so…not Brady. Brady was the even-keeled one who never lost his temper. When Dev or Cody raged, when Jamison got too high-handed, when Gage didn't take things seriously enough and Tucker was too quiet, there was always Brady ready and willing to bring the disparate parts together to create a unit. There wasn't a dark side to Brady.

She'd never thought.

But this was…uncomfortable. Like realizing you hadn't known someone at all. He was fierce, angry, and just barely tethering his temper…all completely visible in his expression and his demeanor. It was like he'd become someone else altogether.

"I needed to let everyone in on what's going on so Rachel isn't caught in the crosshairs—"

Rachel made a noise as if to interrupt, but Cecilia kept right on talking, not giving her a chance to object. "There was a vague threat at the rez. She wasn't safe there, and no matter who drove her here or picked her up, they were going to get a target too. Elijah knows I took Mak, and he might not know where, but everyone I care about is going to be suspect. So everyone needs to know what's going on, but I need to go back to the rez and my job. If Elijah wants to follow me there, he can go right ahead."

"No," Brady said, as if he had *any* say in the matter.

"I think I'll make my own dec—"

"No," Brady repeated.

Cecilia couldn't physically react what with holding a baby and Grandma Pauline holding the bag of frozen peas to her face. So, she could only do her best to come off as dismissive and haughty.

"And you have some big, bad reason for telling *me* no as if you have any right?"

Still, none of that darkness clicked off. There was no calm, blank demeanor like she expected. Brady Wyatt was visibly, unrelentingly *angry*.

Cecilia found that amazing fact undercut her own anger at his high-handedness. Had she ever seen Brady react to anything with this edgy fury? What was causing it? Why did it make her heart flutter?

"Elijah Jones is a sociopath," Brady ground out. "And a murderer, though I've never been able to prove it. He's Ace's protégé in every way, and he's spent the past eight years screwing with me, in particular, because I had the misfortune of being the first Wyatt to arrest him. My first arrest."

"You know this Elijah," Jamison said, his voice deceptively calm. Cecilia didn't believe that calm for one second. "A Sons member, who idolizes our father, targeted you. And this is the first we're hearing about it? Some eight years later?"

Brady was quiet for a long while, some of his normal stoicism clicking into place as he stood there. But his hand was still clenched in a fist at his side. "I think he would have settled for any Wyatt," Brady said after a while, purposefully ignoring Jamison's question. "I got lucky."

"How?" Jamison demanded.

"Pranks, mostly. Threats, sometimes. Nothing concrete and nothing dangerous. It was just like being taunted. It's why I didn't tell you. It was nothing. Just annoying."

"Why?" Tucker asked quietly. "What's the motivation? Ace is in jail. There's no need to win his favor by screwing with one of his sons."

No matter who asked the question, Cecilia couldn't seem to tear her gaze away from Brady.

"I couldn't say. If I understood it, I would have already dealt with it, or told you all about it," Brady said. With every word he was locking down those pieces of his usual calm. The fire in his eyes banked, the tension in his arms released. He was still intense, but the anger had disappeared. Or he'd hidden it.

"He hasn't visited Ace," Jamison said. "If he's some kind of protégé there hasn't been a connection since Ace has been in jail."

Cecilia sighed. "He's not looking to *be* Ace. He's looking to *replace* Ace. He wants to lead the Sons." She let her finger trace Mak's cheek. "If he's targeting a Wyatt, it's not for Ace so much as Wyatts are the Sons' enemy. You guys are the biggest threat to the Sons right now. You took down Ace and Tony. They've been scrambling."

"Eight years," Jamison said gravely. "That hasn't been true for the eight years he's been harassing Brady."

"True. Maybe there's something more to it. I can't speak to that. I didn't know he'd been harassing Brady either. What I do know is that Elijah wants to take over the Sons. It's why he started recruiting on the rez. The more people he enlists, the more power he has in the group itself."

"Why didn't he start his own?" Dev demanded.

"Why start your own when you can take over one of the biggest, most dangerous gangs in the country? I'm not saying it's always been his plan. I'm just saying things changed when Ace was arrested. Elijah's been different the past few months—around the rez, with Mak's mom. He's already got his own little group. It's not enough for him. He wants the Sons." Cecilia looked down at Mak in her arms. He'd started to doze there, immune to the tension around him. "But first, he'll want *his* son."

Which was why she had to leave. Any security could be breached if there was a constant, determined effort to get through. If Cecilia stayed, Elijah would only work on it until he breached it—which wouldn't just put Mak in danger, but Grandma Pauline, her sons, the Knights and any of the little ones.

Cecilia couldn't stick around. And she couldn't let anyone know she was getting out and leading Elijah away. They wouldn't let her.

But the sooner she disappeared, the better off everyone would be.

So, she let the Wyatts and the Knights argue it out, and she kept her gaze and her attention on Mak in her arms. If it was going to be the last time she saw him, held him, she was going to soak it all up.

"So, it's settled then," Jamison said, always the de facto leader. "Everyone stays put until we have a better read on what Elijah Jones is planning, or even better, until we can find a reason to arrest him."

Cecilia tore her gaze from Mak and found Brady's. The anger was back, but he didn't argue with Jamison. He just stared right back at her as if he knew what she was planning.

But he couldn't, and even if he did, he wouldn't stop her.

No one would.

Chapter Seven

"She's going to bolt." Brady found himself pacing. He'd already not felt like himself for months now, but these past few days had taken away all his usual coping mechanisms. All the filters and layers he put over his true feelings so he wasn't...

Well, his father.

This morning was worse. Everyone seemed content to just hang around Grandma Pauline's, pay extra attention to Cody's security measures, and wait.

They couldn't just *wait*. Cecilia would do something stupid. She was too rash. Too...her. She was going to try to lead Elijah away and Brady seemed to be the only one who realized it.

"Cecilia knows better," Tucker insisted, shoveling eggs into his mouth. He was sitting at Grandma Pauline's kitchen table dressed for his work as a detective. Slacks and a button-up shirt. Though he didn't live at the ranch, he would be staying close just like everyone else while they tried to protect Mak from Elijah.

"She most certainly does not," Brady returned. "Are you even listening to yourself?"

"She's a cop."

"She's a..." Brady didn't say "loose cannon" out loud because it sounded like a bad line from some '80s action movie, but she was.

She always had been.

"I think you're underestimating her," Tucker said, with just enough condescension Brady ground his teeth together.

Still, he bit back the words he wanted to say. Because *no, you are* was childish, even if it was true.

If no one would listen to him, he'd have to take matters into his own hands. He gave half a thought to trying to lure Elijah away himself, but Brady didn't think Elijah would go for it. Cecilia had been the one to take Mak. Cecilia would be his target. Elijah was too smart to think Brady was doing anything except setting a trap.

Which meant Brady had to get Cecilia and Mak away from here—without Elijah being any the wiser.

"How's the shoulder?" Tuck asked around another mouthful of eggs.

"Fine," Brady replied without thinking about it. He gave it a little shrug. He had to admit, it hadn't been paining him as much lately. Maybe the third round of antibiotics had actually done what they were supposed to.

"When's your next doctor's appointment?"

Brady gave Tucker a puzzled frown over his sudden interest in doctor appointments. "Next week."

Tuck nodded. "Then I'd make sure you don't miss

it," Tucker said blandly, moving away from the table. He took his plate to the sink and rinsed it, and left the kitchen without another word.

Brady frowned after him. It had been a subtle *don't go anywhere*. As if by being subtle, Brady wouldn't read the subtext and be irritated his younger brother was trying to tell him what to do.

Grandma Pauline breezed in, a basket of eggs hooked to one arm. She gave Brady a critical look. "You're not so peaked looking."

High praise, Brady figured. "I'm doing better."

"Good," she said firmly. "Now, when are you going?"

"Going?"

"Don't think I can't see through you, boy. And that hardheaded woman. You've both got it in your head to hightail it out of here. Neither of you can let the other do it alone. So. When do you sneak out?"

"I…" He could lie to his grandmother. He'd done it before. It just so rarely worked, and she seemed approving. "I was just going to stop her when she did, then convince her the three of us should—"

"No, you'll leave the boy here," Grandma interrupted matter-of-factly.

"But—"

"The safest place for that boy is here, especially if both you and Cecilia take off. Just like when we had Brianna while Cody and Nina were off."

"Only because they got ambushed on their way back from the jail, Grandma. They wouldn't have left Brianna by choice." When Ace had sent men to threaten Nina and Brianna, Nina had come to Cody for help. They'd been separated from their daughter and trying to survive Ace's men, but not because they'd chosen to be.

"They would have left her with me, and would still, if it was the best way to keep her safe," Grandma returned, as if that was just fact, not her opinion. "And Brianna was older. She could hide and be quiet. This little one can't do that. And you can't move fast enough carrying formula and diapers and a crib. Not if you're going to catch her."

"Catch her?"

Grandma Pauline rolled her eyes. "You don't think that girl is already making plans? She's not going to wait to skulk away under the dark of night. She would have done that last night, if so. My guess is she's going to come up with an excuse to run to town, make sure no one goes with her, and hightail it from there."

Brady stared dumbfounded for a moment, because of course that was exactly what Cecilia was going to do. He'd expected more subterfuge, but she hardly needed it when she was an adult woman who would need to do some things without supervision.

"Packed you a bag."

Brady blinked at his grandmother. "Why didn't you kick up a fuss last night? Tell them that their plan was wrong?"

"What's the point in arguing with all you fools?

You're going to do whatever you want anyway. You take that truck Liza borrowed. Bag is packed with supplies. Don't you let that girl out of your sight. You can each take care of yourself, there ain't no doubt about that. But this is dangerous, which means you need to take care of each other. And trust us to take care of the little one."

It was hardly the first time in his life his grandmother had helped him, or seen through him or the rest of them. It was hardly the first time she'd known exactly what to say, and when to say it. He'd been blessed to have her for these twenty years he'd been free of the Sons.

Brady pressed a kiss to his grandmother's cheek. "I know you don't like to hear it, but we would have been lost without you. Lost. Separate. Maybe like him."

Grandma only grunted and shooed him away. "Not one of you has got it in you to be like him, not truly. Be better off if you believe that. Now go."

TIMING WAS EVERYTHING when a person was planning their unapproved escape.

Okay, escape was maybe an exaggeration. Cecilia wasn't being held *prisoner*. She was just trying to avoid her family's arguments.

So, that morning, Cecilia waited until Duke and Sarah were out with the cattle. Cody, Nina and Brianna had stayed at the Knight ranch last night to put up some extra security measures, but Nina and

Brianna had gone over to the Wyatts' this morning so Gigi and Brianna could have their homeschool lessons. Cody was currently installing something on the entrance gate. All Cecilia had to do was wait to hear Rachel turn on the water to the shower, and she could slip out.

They'd decided it safest if Mak stayed at the Wyatt ranch, since they already had a crib and a few baby supplies that Brady had brought in with his backpack. There wasn't anything at the Knights', so it would have required bringing baby things in and out—which could have been detected by anyone who might be watching.

Cecilia could have spent the night at the Wyatts', but she'd decided to say her goodbyes last night. That way she could get a handle on her emotions for today. Today required strength of spirit, not doubts born of the selfish need to be with Mak.

A quick note, a careful route across the property to the back exit—avoiding the pastures Duke and Sarah were in today—and she was home free.

Her gut twisted at the idea of causing her family worry, but worry was better than harm. No amount of words or arguments would allow them to accept Elijah's prime target was *her*, which meant she needed to be far away.

So, as she'd learned to do as a teenager, instead of fighting the brick wall of a united Wyatt-Knight front, she'd sneak away and do the thing she knew was right.

She *knew* it was right. If only she was in danger, maybe she'd agree with her family. Teamwork was better than going off on your own.

But it wasn't about her. It was about Mak.

So, Cecilia wrote her letter. She decided not to leave it in the kitchen, just because it would set the alarm too quickly. She needed a head start so they didn't think they could come after her.

Mailbox. Perfect. She'd slip it in on her way out. Duke or Sarah didn't usually head out that way until the end of the day. Plenty of time.

Satisfied with her plan, she slung her bag over her shoulder and slid the letter into her pocket. If she happened to get caught, she'd just pretend she was taking some stuff for Mak over to the Wyatt ranch. Then she'd try again tomorrow.

She heard the groan of pipes as Rachel started the shower. She took a deep breath and reminded herself she knew she was right. This was the right thing for Mak and that was all that mattered.

She slid out the door as quietly as she could. Keeping her eyes on the horizon on the off chance Sarah or Duke would unexpectedly come back to the house before lunch. Or one of Dev's dogs—he'd insisted Sarah start keeping them with her—might start barking.

Nothing. She moved quickly and stealthily to the other side of the house where her truck was parked— purposefully away from views of the doors or windows.

But she stopped short when she turned the corner and spotted Brady leaning negligently against the hood of her truck.

He tipped down his sunglasses, clearly made a mental note of her bag, and then smiled. "Going somewhere?"

For a few full seconds all Cecilia could do was gape. Surely…this was a coincidence. He wasn't sitting there because he knew what she was up to.

She kept walking toward her truck, trying to keep the suspicion out of her tone. "Just gotta run some errands. I left in kind of a hurry yesterday," she said, trying to sound casual.

Brady gestured to the tinted out truck Liza had driven to the ranch. He'd parked it behind hers so she couldn't back out. "I'll drive you."

She frowned, clutching the strap of her bag. "Why would you do that?"

"You can't get very far on that doughnut tire, and I'm assuming you want to go a little farther than the rez."

He laid that accusation so casually, she almost agreed. She caught herself in time, harnessing her indignation that he'd clearly seen through her. "I don't know what you're talking about."

"Sure," he agreed easily. "But I'll drive you all the same."

"I don't need a chauffeur, Brady. Go back to the ranch and rest up that bum shoulder of yours."

He rolled the shoulder in question, then shrugged. "Feels plenty rested to me. Think I kicked that infection this time around. Isn't that handy?" He gestured at her. "Might be kind of hard to see around that swollen eye. Probably be better if I drive."

She didn't know what to do with…whatever he was doing. The way he was acting. "Did you and Gage switch bodies or something? Is that why Felicity jumped ship so quick?"

"Careful," he warned, and his tone had an edge to it that reminded her of last night when he'd been so *angry*.

His expression was calm, though. And she felt two inches tall for making a comment about Felicity's old crush on Brady, when it was clear to anyone who paid half a second of attention she genuinely loved Gage.

"Go away, Brady," Cecilia said, her control slipping. This was hard enough without having to fight him. "I've got stuff to do, and it's got nothing to do with you."

"That'd be easy, wouldn't it? But we both know it isn't true."

"Whatever," she muttered. She wasn't going to argue with him. She was going to get in her truck and leave.

She stalked toward the door. Brady stepped in front of it. Her temper snapped and she gave him a shove.

He didn't budge.

"I'm not afraid to hurt you, Brady," she seethed through gritted teeth.

"Try me."

The arrogance in his tone had her lashing out without thinking the move through. He dodged the elbow she almost landed on his gut, then grabbed her arm and moved it behind her back like he was getting ready to cuff her.

Her temper didn't just snap now, it ignited. She kicked out, landed a blow to his shin, which weakened his grip. She wrenched her arm away and swung.

He blocked the blow, feinted left well enough she fell for it. Then he had both her wrists in his grasp and held them against the truck behind her so she was trapped.

They both breathed heavily and Cecilia didn't fight the hold. She could get out of it, but as much as she didn't have any qualms about sparring with Brady, she didn't feel right about actually hurting him—which she would have to do to escape his grip.

She took a deep breath, tried to turn the fire of fury inside of her into ice. She angled her chin toward his wounded shoulder. "I could get out of this in five seconds flat if I fought dirty." Even if he was finally healing, one well-placed strike to his wound would have him on his knees.

He didn't even blink or wince. "Not if I fought dirty right back."

"You?" She snorted, even though his hands were curled around her wrists and his body was way, way, *way* too close to hers. She could feel his body heat, and he didn't have to be touching her anywhere but her wrists to get the sense of just how big and strong he was.

And this was really not to the time to wonder what it would feel like if he *was* touching her anywhere else.

Except, then that's exactly what he did. Inch by inch, he pinned his body to hers—her back against the metal door of her truck, her front against...him. And she wasn't sure which was a harder, less giving surface.

It was meant to be threatening, maybe. A show of power, and that he was bigger and stronger than she was. But she didn't think it had any of the desired effects, because what she really wanted to do was press right back. Even with his hands tight around her wrists.

Brady's face was too close, and he had that fierceness from last night that, God help her, it really did something for her. She liked he had some secret edge. That he wasn't perfect or so easily contained.

Which was not at all what she should be thinking about. She should be fighting dirty. Getting out of his hold, even if it meant hurting him. But she couldn't bring herself to.

"He knows you took Mak," Brady said, his voice a razor's edge against the quiet morning. "I get it. He's not going to stop until he figures out what you did with him. But his men also followed me and Liza. Maybe they gave up, but Elijah has some unknown beef with me too. We're in the same boat. Stay, we lead him to Mak. It can't happen. But if we leave? We lead Elijah away."

Cecilia had to swallow to speak, to focus on his words instead of the heat spreading through her. The throbbing deep inside of her. "Just what are you suggesting?" she managed to demand. Or squeak. She wasn't sure which sound actually came out of her mouth.

"That we do this together, Cecilia. Lead Elijah away, and take him on. While having each other's back."

Chapter Eight

There was a faint buzzing in Brady's head, and he was having a hard time not letting it take over. If it won, this wouldn't be about Elijah or danger or anything else. It would be about *them*.

But today wasn't about the surprisingly soft woman he was currently pressing against a truck. Today was about keeping Mak safe. Keeping Cecilia safe.

Seriously, *why* had he pushed her against the truck? To prove some point that he was physically stronger? He was well aware Cecilia could hold her own if she was giving it a full 100 percent. She had gone easy on him in their little tussle because of his shoulder, just like he'd gone easy on her because neither of them wanted to actually *hurt* each other.

So, why was he crowding her against the truck as his body rioted with…reaction? A heat that *should* have warned him of danger. He shouldn't want to lean into it, explore it.

Relish it.

He realized belatedly he was leaning in, getting

closer. He could smell her, feel her. What would it matter if he—

That just could not happen. He was *not* this person.

He released her abruptly. Which wasn't his best move. It showed her way more than he wanted to admit. He stopped himself from scraping his hands over his face. Stopped himself from gulping for air like he wanted to. He tried to picture himself encased in ice so any and all further reactions were frozen deep inside of him.

What was wrong with him? He felt like there was some rogue part of himself sprouting up and refusing to be caged away like it usually was.

He wasn't attracted to Cecilia. She irritated him. She challenged him. That *infuriated* him—it didn't make him want her. This was simply an aberration. A...hallucination.

Something real and enticing for the first time in a long time.

Which didn't matter. Not now. What mattered was outwitting Elijah.

"Get in the truck, Cecilia," he managed to say, without sounding like he felt. Raked over coals. Shaken until his brain was mush. "Or we'll be found out before we leave the ranch."

Cecilia stood there, still pressed to the truck like she was afraid to move. Which was ridiculous. Cecilia was never afraid. Certainly not of him. She'd fought right back when he'd tried to stop her from getting in her truck.

But he could see her pulse rioting in her neck. She breathed unevenly, lips slightly parted. And she didn't move.

Everything inside of him *ached* with something he refused to acknowledge or name.

"No one else knows?" she finally asked, her voice more or less a whisper. Infused with suspicion, but a whisper nonetheless.

Brady forced his body to level out. When he spoke, it was controlled. Even. "Grandma Pauline. She's the one who convinced me to go with you, not stop you." And not go on his own. But Cecilia didn't need to know he'd had the same plan as she did. "She said we should leave Mak."

Cecilia visibly swallowed as if that hurt, but she nodded. "He'll be safer here. Away from me."

He could *see* the way that pained her, just like he could feel an echoing of that same pain inside of him. There was something about taking care of Mak that had crawled inside of him, lodged somewhere near his heart.

"He'll be safer away from us," Brady corrected, because he needed the verbal reminder himself. "It might not connect, but I'm Elijah's target too."

Cecilia nodded, as if agreeing. Then she pushed herself off the truck and went to the one with tinted windows that he'd been driving. They both climbed inside in silence, buckled in that same heavy absence of noise.

Brady spared Cecilia a glance as he turned the

key. She had her hands clasped in her lap and she looked straight ahead. Long strands of black hair that had slipped out of her braid framed her face. He'd known her since he'd come to Grandma Pauline's. She was as familiar to him as his brothers, more or less.

But he found himself staring, when he had no business staring. When he had no business being… affected by said staring.

"It'd earn him respect," Cecilia said abruptly. "Elijah. For him to screw with one of those Wyatt brothers who left, who went into law enforcement and thumbed their nose at their father, at the Sons—"

Brady jumped on this thread he could follow without getting as lost as he felt when he was staring at her. "Who got Ace thrown in jail. There are plenty of men in that place who like Ace. Hell, worship Ace. He's the best leader they've ever had. If Elijah takes a chunk out of us, my bet is he gets the respect of those who follow Ace even now." Brady nudged the truck forward, watching the surroundings to make sure they weren't spotted.

"But us leaving together… Doesn't that prove Mak is here? That we left him here?"

"Depends. I think we can make it look like anything, if he doesn't know where Mak is right now. We can make it look like we have him. We can make it look like we've taken him somewhere else. We can even make it look like we split up, so he won't know which thread to follow. He'll have to split resources thinking we're apart, but we'll be together the whole time."

"We," Cecilia echoed. She squeezed her hands together. If it were someone else, he might have attributed that gesture to fear.

"We," Brady said firmly, because at least in that he was sure. "Whatever his reasons, Elijah's targeting us both right now. He followed us both. So it's a we. I want to keep Mak safe as much as you do."

"Is it that bad?" She squeezed her eyes shut and shook her head. "I don't know why I even asked that. Of course growing up in a gang is *that bad*."

"I wouldn't know it was that bad if I hadn't gotten out. I knew it was… Wrong isn't the right word, because when you have nothing else it's not wrong. It didn't fit, though. It didn't seem right. And Jamison, well, he could remember living with Mom at Grandma Pauline's. He'd had that glimpse of different. He made us all believe in it. Believe we deserved it. Mak wouldn't have that."

Cecilia inhaled sharply. "Would it have been different? If you didn't have Jamison?"

She'd never know how often he'd asked himself that. How often he'd wondered if Jamison was the reason he'd followed the straight and narrow against the bad that must be inside him. How often he'd hoped it was something deeper, something good inside of *him*.

But he could never be sure. "I'll never know," he said, pulling out onto the gravel road on the back of the Knight property. It would lead them to the highway. And then...

"Where are we going?" She sounded more like herself again. In control and ready to fight whatever came their way.

"That's an excellent question. Got any ideas?"

CECILIA GAPED AT BRADY. "I'm sorry...you don't have a plan?"

He gestured her way, though he kept his gaze on the road. "This is the plan."

"This isn't a plan. It's not even half a plan. It's the teeny tiny beginning of a plan." She forced herself to take a breath so she didn't start sounding panicked, even though that was the exact feeling gripping her throat. "*I* had a plan. You come in and ruin my plan and then... I can't believe you of all people would do something without thinking it through."

"I've thought it through. We find someplace to hunker down. We contact Elijah and see if he'll come after us. Then we work together to arrest him."

"*Someplace* is not a plan. *See if* is not a plan!"

Brady rolled his eyes. "We'll work it out. Do you think my apartment is far enough away?"

"No. Besides, too many innocent bystanders in an apartment building. Same with my place. Too close to neighbors he could use."

"And where were *you* going to go?" Brady asked loftily.

"Motels. Crisscross around. Make it look like I'm

running, trying to lose him." She threw Brady a con-descending glance that he didn't see since his eyes were on the road. "You can't contact him. That's too obvious."

Brady shrugged negligently. "I think Elijah runs toward the obvious."

"Maybe. But he doesn't think *we* will. He reacts to fear." Cecilia looked out of the windshield at the highway flying by, the rolling hills, patches of brown from the fading summer heat against the green, slowly morphing into the landscape of the Bad-lands. Rock outcroppings in the distance that would take over the whole horizon. She thought of the dead prairie dog, the dead raccoon, the simple notes. "He wants me afraid. If we act like we're running, he'll take the bait. Though I wouldn't mind leaving a few dead animals for *him* to find, I think acting like we're on the losing side is what we should do."

"He left you dead animals?" Brady asked, and for a second she was fooled by the deadly calm in his voice, so she simply shrugged.

"That's serial killer behavior."

She turned at the cold edge of fury in his voice. It was mesmerizing, seeing anger on Brady. She knew he'd been angry before. It wasn't that she'd ever been truly fooled by the careful armor he placed over him-self. It was just she couldn't understand why it had broken down *now*. The Wyatts had been through some bad things the past few months.

Maybe it was the gunshot wound, and the infections. Just frustration bubbling over. Maybe it had nothing to do with this.

With you.

Uncomfortable with that thought, she pushed it away and focused on what he'd said rather than how he'd said it. "Like you pointed out last night, he's a sociopath. Though I don't fully understand how so many sociopaths can congregate in one group, follow one leader. How do people like Elijah and Ace get whole swaths of men following them? Willing to kill for them?"

"They normalize each other's behavior and lack of feelings. That's how groups like the Sons form. People with all sorts of mental problems normalized by each other, exacerbated by each other. They're told the outside is the enemy. If they're miserable, if they're poor, if they've been hurt—the outside is the reason for it. The outside is the reason they're miserable, and if they strike out enough they'll finally be safe and happy."

It made a sad kind of sense.

"But make no mistake, Cecilia, people like Ace and Elijah are worse. They know what they're doing. They know how to manipulate people. Maybe they have their own warped view that the world has harmed them, so they have to harm the world, but there's nothing to feel sorry for."

"Did you mistake me for someone with sympathy?"

He flicked a glance her way. "You aren't without sympathy."

"You know how it is. You're a cop long enough, it starts to eat away at you. Hard to watch people make bad decisions over and over for no good reason and not develop a certain kind of cynicism." She wasn't sure why she said that. She wasn't in a habit of admitting her cynicism—though she knew Brady would understand, would have to. He'd been a cop a few years longer than she had, and he didn't have the same connection to the people he served as she did.

"I think everything you did for your friend, and for Mak, proves that whatever you might feel on a bad day isn't who you actually are. That's not a criticism. If you lose all your humanity, badge or no, you're no different than Ace or Elijah."

The way he said it had her stomach twisting painfully. "Do you worry about that?"

He stared hard at the road, his grip on the steering wheel tightening before she watched him carefully relax it. "Sometimes."

"You shouldn't. I don't know a better man than you, Brady."

"Duke," he replied automatically, trying to defer the attention to someone else, it was clear.

"Duke's a great man," Cecilia agreed. She didn't like feeling soft, didn't like this need to soothe. But Brady brought it out in her, because she knew a lot of men and Brady *was* the best. Whether he wanted to believe that or not. "He's a wonderful father or father figure. But he's a crusty cowboy with a chip on his shoulder who still hasn't quite accepted his daughters are grown women. Jamison is like that too—he looks at all of you, and all of us like we're still kids. It doesn't make them bad people, it just... Well, you don't do that."

He shifted uncomfortably, like he didn't know what to do with the praise. She doubted any of the Wyatt men were particularly used to having nice things being said to their faces. Grandma Pauline was amazing—but she wasn't *complimentary*.

"I guess that's just being the middle child. One foot in each door. Understanding the oldest side and the younger sides." He slid her a look. "Or maybe not, since technically you're in the middle and you still treat Rachel and Sarah like babies who need protecting."

Cecilia frowned. "I do not."

"Okay."

She stared at him in shock. He was *patronizing* her. "Don't *okay* me. I do not treat them like babies!" She was being *nice*, and he was turning on her. The jerk.

"You're right," he added, with almost enough contrition to mollify her. "You treat them, and Felicity, come to think of it, more like toddlers than babies."

Her mouth dropped in outrage. She couldn't believe Brady was criticizing her. And over how she treated her sisters. Which was not any of his business, and certainly not an area he was an expert on. "I was being *nice* to you."

"Yeah, and I'm telling you the truth," he replied, still so casual as if they weren't arguing at all. "Which you know is the truth or you wouldn't be pissed off." He nodded toward the road sign for the next three towns. "You have a motel in mind?"

Cecilia crossed her arms over her chest, tried not to feel petulant. She did *not* treat her sisters like toddlers. She was just protective of them, because she knew all the awful that was out in the world. Who cared if Brady understood that or not? They had far bigger problems at hand. "The Mockingbird in Dyner."

Brady winced, but nodded. "All right. Hope you brought your hazmat suit."

Chapter Nine

Brady drove toward the scummy motel Cecilia had named. It wouldn't have been his choice, but he understood Cecilia's thinking. They had to look like they were trying to evade notice. A cash-only, by-the-hour motel room would be just the place. He'd have to put his comfort aside.

The trick was going to be to get Elijah himself to come after them. He likely had a never-ending supply of men who'd take orders under the right incentives or threats. Brady figured they could fight off attacks, as long as Elijah didn't know where Mak was, but that would be the constant, overwhelming worry.

Brady slowed the truck about a block away from the Mockingbird. He turned to Cecilia, who was still pouting by his estimation. He didn't know why that *amused* him. It should be irritating or frustrating or *nothing*, but something about tough, extreme Cecilia pouting over being called overprotective made him want to laugh.

This was very much not the time or place for that, so he focused on the task at hand. "I think you should go in there alone. We should try to make it look like you're running away by yourself. We're more likely to lure him out that way."

Cecilia blinked at him. "That's what *I* was going to say."

"Then we're on the same page."

She turned in her seat to face him, to study him as though she were somehow confused by their agreement. "You're not going to pull the macho you-need-a-man-to-protect-you card?"

"No, in part because you don't need a man—you just need a partner. But also in part because, if Elijah is anything like Ace, he thinks less of women. Which means you being on your own is going to be impossible for him to resist. It won't occur to him he could be beaten by a woman. He's more likely to go after you, most especially if he thinks you're alone."

She nodded grimly. "True enough. So, I'll walk the last block, and you'll stay here. Can you do that?"

He nodded, though the idea of her walking that last block on her own made him edgy. "You'll have to watch for anyone who might be following you. Have your phone and your gun and—"

She rolled her eyes. "*Duh*, Brady."

"Duh. Really?"

She shook her head, digging through her backpack to pull out a holster. She slid her gun inside. "I'll walk over and check in. I'm thinking you should stay here till dark so no one at the hotel sees you."

Brady glanced at the clock. No, that'd be too much

time. "You'll text me the room number and leave the rest up to me."

"We want everyone to think I'm alone so no hotel employees can give us away if Elijah or his men come sniffing around. You're hardly inconspicuous."

"What does that mean?"

"You're—" she waved a hand at him, from his head to his foot on the brake "—big."

He raised an eyebrow.

"Come on. You're all Wyatt. Tall and broad and it isn't going to take a genius to put it together. There's no mistaking a Wyatt."

He didn't like it, but she was probably right. Much as he'd rather not admit it, he and his brothers all looked like Ace. Whoever Elijah sent would be able to put it together pretty easily even if they'd never seen Brady.

"He's after both of us. Maybe we both—"

"Don't start second-guessing just because you want to protect me, Brady. You were right the first time. If he thinks I'm alone we're more likely to get Elijah."

"It's not about wanting to protect." He wasn't sure what it *was* about, but surely he was more evolved than that.

"My butt." She slid out of the truck. "Wait until dark," Cecilia insisted before quietly closing the door.

He did not like being told what to do, and liked even less the high-handed way she'd ended any more discussion on the matter. They were supposed to be partners, working together.

Even if he'd all but forced her into that. Still, she'd *agreed*. Which meant they had to agree on the next courses of action. Teams *agreed* on what they were doing.

He could have gotten out of the truck and followed her. He could have driven over to the parking lot. There were a great many things he *could* do— she wasn't in charge of him.

But they'd come up with this plan, and he knew it was the best one. Even if it bothered him, on a deep, cellular, not-intellectual level that she was walking by herself, getting a room by herself. He wouldn't even know if she'd been intercepted.

He tightened his grip on the steering wheel and tried to talk himself out of all the worst-case scenarios. But worst-case scenarios existed because sometimes the worst case did.

He didn't have to blow their plan to bits to try and mitigate some potential worst cases. He'd parked on the curb of a pretty deserted street. Empty storefronts, a few with broken windows on the higher stories. There were two cars parked on the street—one in front of him, and one behind. Both were rusted severely, and one had a flat tire, so they likely hadn't moved in a while.

If he backtracked, there was a narrow alley. He could fit the truck back there, and as long as he made sure the buildings on either side were empty, and it looked like the alley was unused, he could park there without being noticed.

Then he could sneak up to the motel behind the building. Check things out and see if Cecilia had anyone watching her. He hadn't spotted a tail on the drive over, so he was pretty sure they hadn't been found yet.

Satisfied with his plan, he took a circular route to the alley—still no tail, and there weren't many places for one to hide in this deserted part of Dyner. He parked the truck, searched the alley for signs of use, and when he found none, settled his bag on his shoulder and started walking toward the motel.

It was easy to go around back and avoid the parking lot. The motel was a small, old, bedraggled building. It was squat but long, and separated into two sides of rooms with the main office at the end. The back of the buildings abutted a small copse of scraggly-looking trees.

Brady used the trees as cover as he moved toward the motel. From the back it was just a slab of concrete with the tiniest of squares in each unit that were bleary windows that didn't look like they'd been cleaned in decades.

The two sections of rooms were split by a breezeway in the middle. Brady stopped and watched the narrow space. It would have taken Cecilia some time to not just walk up to the motel office, but also check in. If Brady stayed put and watched the breezeway and Cecilia passed, he'd know her room was on the east side. If she didn't pass after a certain amount of time, she was likely on the west side.

Unless she'd already gone to her room. But just as he was considering that possibility, Cecilia walked briskly past the breezeway.

He moved out of the woods, careful and alert to the potential of being watched. He moved through the breezeway, looked out just in time to see Cecilia step into the last unit.

He retraced his steps to the back of the building, moved down the length of the east side until he reached the end. He sent her a text telling her to unlock the door.

Her response was about what he expected.

I told you to stay put.

So he repeated his previous text: Unlock the door.

She didn't reply to that one. He moved around the corner, watching the entire area around him for someone who might be watching the door Cecilia had gone into. She hadn't just left it unlocked, she'd left it ajar.

He slid inside.

She closed and locked the door behind him, and while her stance was calm, her eyes were fury personified.

"I told you to wait."

"It was too long to wait. I could have just as easily been spotted in that truck. I haven't seen any tails or any signs of being watched. Have you?"

She frowned. "No."

"They haven't figured us out yet."

"That only means they're hanging around the ranches. I don't like that."

"Neither do I, but you yourself said we can't contact Elijah and lure him out. He has to think we're on the run." Brady looked around the room. It smelled like stale cigarette smoke and mildew. He was sure the bedding hadn't been updated since 1990, at best. Everything had a vague layer of grime over it.

"I gave a fake name at the desk," Cecilia said, pacing the small patch of threadbare carpet. "They didn't ask for my ID."

"He'll be looking for someone with your description, not your name."

"I know." She hugged her arms around herself. "I just hate that while we wait for him to find us, he's going to be harassing our families."

"Cody will have that covered."

She didn't say anything to that, but he could read her doubts. There was no way to assuage them. He had doubts of his own. No matter that Cody had trained with the CIA and been part of a secret group who's purpose was to take down the Sons, no amount of security could protect everyone 100 percent. Not long-term.

So, they had to focus on the short term. "Tomorrow, we'll head east. I'll check in at the next motel and you'll hang out in the truck till the coast is clear. We'll switch off like that—in different directions,

buying two or three days in the motels and only staying one. I think he'll follow you, but if he sends some
men after me, it'll split his resources."

"You're not in charge here, Brady. You can't just
stomp in and order me around."

"I wasn't ordering, and I most definitely wasn't
stomping."

She crossed her arms over her chest and lifted her
chin. "Weren't you?"

"Is there a problem with my plan?"

She made a face—pursed lips, wrinkled nose,
frustration personified. "No," she ground out, clearly
irritated.

"Well, then."

"You're infuriating," she said disgustedly.

"I don't see how."

"You're a Wyatt. You wouldn't." She plopped herself on the edge of the bed. She sat there like that,
looking irritable and pouty. After a few moments
it changed. She looked around the room, then narrowed her eyes at him.

After a few more seconds, she smiled, and boy
did he not trust that smile.

There was no way to fight Brady when he was right.
No one was onto them yet, so it made sense he'd
come into the room. Moving to another motel tomorrow and doing the same thing, only with Brady
being the one to check in made sense too.

It would work better if they split up, but that would

leave them both in danger. It made more sense to be partners in this.

But if he was going to irritate her, she had the right to irritate him right back. So, she smiled. "Guess we're gonna share a bed tonight." Because if there was one way to *really* make Brady uncomfortable it was to acknowledge that little spark of heat between them.

"No."

"Afraid I'm going to take advantage of you?" she asked sweetly.

His eyes darkened, and it was probably warped, but she shivered a little. She could picture it just a little too easily. Especially now that he'd pinned her to the truck and she'd felt his body against hers.

What she knew now, that she hadn't known or fully believed back on New Year's Eve, was that he felt it too. That undercurrent of attraction. She wasn't sure she'd ever felt a buzz quite that potent. She'd always assumed she was immune to that—something about being a cop, being tougher and harder than most of her past boyfriends. They'd all liked the *idea* of her, but in practice it had never worked.

No man wanted a superior. At best they wanted an equal.

Brady is definitely equal.

"We shouldn't both sleep at the same time, Cecilia. That's just common sense."

Oh, she hated that *reasonable, condescending* tone. More annoying, the fact he was right when she was just trying to get under his skin. There really *was* something wrong with her thinking he was so attractive when he was equally as obnoxious.

There was something really pathetic about the urge to needle him when she should let it go. So, he hadn't listened and stayed in the truck. She had no doubt he'd evaded any kind of detection. Everything was as fine as it could be under the circumstances.

But she wanted to poke at him until he exploded— until she saw some of that reaction she'd seen last night when he'd been angry and incapable of controlling it.

Apparently he was having the same kind of thoughts.

"Would calling the ranch and checking in make you feel better? Check in on your babies—I mean sisters?"

He asked it so blandly she might have missed the direct dig. She might have even let it go if it didn't make her think she was having the same effect on him that he was having on her. That edginess that left each other incapable of acting reasonably.

When they *had* to act reasonably. They had to focus on the danger they were in, and first and foremost, keeping Mak safe. "I do not treat them like they're babies, but maybe I should treat you like you're one. Or just a cranky five-year-old in need of a nap."

"It was just a joke, Cecilia," he said in a bored tone. "Let it go."

Which of course meant she couldn't. "I will not let it go. I do not treat them that way. If I'm a little protective, it's because *I'm* a cop."

He rolled his eyes. *Rolled. His. Eyes.* "Okay."

She jumped up. "You don't understand because you Wyatts are all cops. So you don't have to worry about any of you being naive." She winced a little. "Or were cops." A reference to Dev whose injuries had ended his police career after just a few months on the job.

"What does it matter if I think you treat your sisters like toddlers?"

It didn't. Not at all. But he was purposefully goading her. And she had to be the bigger person. She had to let it go. "It doesn't matter. At all, in fact."

"There you go." Then he reached out and patted her on the head.

Patted her. On the head.

She poked him square in the chest, which was quite the feat when what she really wanted to do was deck him. "Don't *pat* me on the head, you pompous jerk."

"Don't *poke* me," he returned, taking her wrist and pulling her hand away from his chest. But each finger that wrapped around her narrow wrist was like fire.

It was ridiculous and so over-the-top potent, this thing between them. And it was just going to keep happening. Trying to lure Elijah toward them while working together—spending nights in the same room together—the fights would get old, and they would all end in this. Attraction was going to keep leaping up until they dealt with it head-on. One way or another.

She met his gaze. "We can't pretend this away, Brady."

He dropped her wrist, his armor clicking into place clear as day. "Watch me."

Chapter Ten

Pretend. Brady didn't have to pretend anything away, because this…thing between them was nothing more than weird timing and circumstance. It was just an illusion made up of frustration and fear and danger.

If there was some teeny tiny ember of attraction, it could be easily stomped out.

Once she stopped poking at him.

Why he'd expect her to do that was beyond him. Cecilia was not someone who stepped back from any kind of challenge. She met them head-on. She said things like *we can't pretend this away.*

But clearly she had no clue who she was talking to, because there were a great many things he could pretend away. *This* included. *This* was at the top of the list.

He pulled his phone out of his pocket and dialed Cody. "Need to check in," he muttered to Cecilia without looking her way.

He didn't watch for her response, so if she had one, it wasn't verbal. When Cody answered, Brady kept his greeting short.

"What's the status?"

"You can't be serious."

"Why not?"

Cody sighed. "You just took off. You and Cecilia. We agreed—"

"We didn't agree on anything. Have you had any incidents?"

Cody muttered something Brady couldn't make out, which was probably for the best. "We've definitely had some people poking around, but it's all been pretty weak. I think they know you guys aren't here, and don't suspect you left Mak. Unless they're biding their time."

"Any word on Elijah himself?"

"No. He's laying low as far as we've been able to figure—without digging too deeply so he might realize we're looking into him. Where are you?"

"Best if you don't know."

"I've been in this exact position," Cody said, his tone serious and grave. "Working together, all of us, was—"

"Something that worked for *your* situation, and it might in the future work for this one. But right now, we have to keep Elijah away from Mak any way we can. This is the best way."

Before Cody could respond, the phone was plucked out of his grasp. He turned to scowl at Cecilia.

She had his phone to her ear and a *screw you* expression on her face. "Cody? Yeah. Listen. Stay away from Elijah. Your priority is Mak. All of you out there—your priority is Mak. You let me and Brady deal with Elijah."

Whatever Cody said in response must not have met with her approval because she clicked the end button and then tossed his cell on the disgusting bed.

"Mature, Cecilia."

"I don't need to be mature, and I don't need your baby brother's approval." She crossed her arms over her chest. "We need Elijah to follow us. That's it."

"Did it occur to you I wasn't seeking approval so much as diplomatically trying to get everyone on the same side without barking out orders?"

She waved a dismissive hand. "We do not have time for every Wyatt and every Knight to get on board. Not right now."

"And if they go after Elijah themselves? You're not the only one who does something just because someone tells them not to."

"They won't," she said, as if she actually believed it. "Not only is it not in anyone's best interest—if they start reaching out to Elijah, it puts us in more danger. He'll build his forces for a Wyatt showdown. If he thinks we're working on our own, we have a better chance. Every one of your brothers will come to that conclusion before they try to take something upon themselves, especially with Mak there to remind them."

She wasn't wrong. His brothers might not approve of the plan, but they wouldn't try to interrupt it unless they could guarantee it didn't put more danger on him and Cecilia. Knowing the Wyatts were involved would no doubt increase the danger, so no matter how they complained about it, they wouldn't interfere unless they had a safe way of doing it.

"You can admit I'm right at any time." She smiled at him, all smug satisfaction. Then she moved closer, a saunter if he had to characterize it. With that same look in her eyes she'd had on New Year's Eve.

She did the same thing too. Moved right up to him and placed her hands on his shoulders like they belonged there.

This time though, he knew. She wasn't drunk. She wasn't joking. She was…probably projecting. Better to irritate him, to come on to him and make him angry, than think about the reality of her life.

Which almost made him feel sorry for her. Almost.

If her hands felt good there, if his system screamed in anticipation, he didn't have to—and in fact wouldn't—react.

But she didn't just leave her hands on his shoulders, she slid them up his neck, locking her fingers behind it. She molded her body to his, and it was that same blazing heat as when he'd backed her up against the truck.

Why did all this make his body tighten when he knew better. *Knew* better. "It's just attraction." He had to say it out loud. He had to hear the words himself. Because there was only one tiny little thread of reason holding him back.

She widened her eyes, all fake innocence. "Gee. I thought it was chaste, attraction-less, pure-hearted happily-ever-after."

He puffed out a breath and reached behind him to pull her arms from around his neck.

She didn't let herself be pulled. In fact, she sort of rolled against him and for a second he was frozen, holding her arms, pressed to her, blood roaring in his head.

What would be the harm?

"It doesn't have to mean anything, Brady," she said, her voice soft. "Consider it a distraction under stress. You're not exactly *unmoved*."

That at least poked holes in the haze of attraction and want, because it was a lie. Because he heard a hint of desperation she was trying so hard to hide. "You think it'd be that easy?" He laughed, though it wasn't a particularly nice laugh. "How naive are you?"

She looked a bit like he'd slapped her, and while that gave him a stab of pain, she had to understand what she was saying. And he had to be kind of a jerk so she'd stop…doing this. "Did you forget about that kiss at New Year's Eve, Cecilia?"

"No."

"It didn't mean anything, so it never occurred to you to think about it again?"

"Brady, I—"

"You kissed me and any attraction that prompted it evaporated. You didn't want to anymore." He gestured to the small space between them. Derisively. "Clearly. It all went away."

She blinked at him, some of that sexy certainty slipping off her face. "That was just a kiss."

"And what you're suggesting is just sex." He unwound her arms from around his neck and she finally released him. "If a kiss lingered, what would sex do?"

"It doesn't have to be like that," she said stubbornly.

"Doesn't it? You've actually slept with someone and all feelings and attraction immediately disappeared?"

Her eyebrows drew together like she was trying to make sense of a foreign language. "Of course."

"Of course? Cecilia, you must have had some spectacularly bad sex." Which was not an easy thing to think when she was still so close. Clearly…missing out.

She bristled. "You have no idea what kind of sex life I've had."

"No. And I don't want to." Not in a million years did he want to imagine what kind of morons she'd been with. "But sex changes things. It's nakedness and intimacy, and that's fine if you're casual friends or you pick someone up at a bar. It's fine if you think you're going to date and see if you're compatible. It's not fine if you're practically family."

"Because you decreed the laws and rules of what's fine and what's not?"

She was the most frustrating woman in the world. He had no idea why that made him want to put his hands on her face, to show her—long, slow, and thoroughly—what a real kiss would do.

Luckily he was distracted from the impulse by the alarm going off on his phone. "I need to change my bandage," he said stiffly, and grabbed his bag and walked into the bathroom, hoping he could leave all *that* behind him.

CECILIA DIDN'T PARTICULARLY enjoy being chastised, or other people being right, but there was something about the way Brady had handled her that made her feel both—chastised and very, very wrong.

She wanted to pout over it, but the predominant feeling—nearly eclipsing the ever-present worry that she couldn't keep Mak safe—was a heavy sadness.

She sat down on the bed and rested her chin in her hands. He wasn't wrong exactly. It was nice to throw herself at him, argue with him, because it didn't leave much room for worry. She could turn that off, and *God* she was desperate to turn that constant, exhausting anxiety off.

There were other ways to argue with Brady. Not such easy ones, but she didn't have to throw herself at him. Especially when he so easily countered all her moves.

You must have had some spectacularly bad sex.

She scowled. What did Brady know? He was uptight and repressed. Sure, he was hot. And that brief moment he'd returned the New Year's Eve kiss had been something like electric, but there was no way Brady wasn't just stern vanilla.

Then I think you're attracted to stern vanilla.

She heard a muttered swear from the bathroom and leaned sideways to see through the crack in the door.

Brady was clearly struggling with removing and bandaging his wound himself. Stubborn mule.

She got to her feet and marched for the tiny bathroom. She inched the door the rest of the way open. "Oh, for heaven's sake. Let me help you."

He scowled at her in the mirror over the sink. "I can do it on my own."

"Not well." She stalked over to him and tugged the alcohol wipe out of his hand. She set to tending the wound, ignoring the fact he was shirtless. She was mad at him, and she wasn't going to soak in the sight of pure *muscle* on display. She was above that. "It looks better." She coughed. "Your wound."

"Antibiotics must have worked this time," he said in that robotic Brady voice that made her want to scream.

Instead she finished disinfecting the area. "That's good."

"It is."

She rolled her eyes at the inane conversation. She pulled the new bandages out of the box on the rusty sink, then pointed to the bed. "Oh, go sit down."

He grunted, but did as he was told. She followed,

noting that the beautifully muscled torso and arms both had their share of scars. "Where'd you get all those?" she asked, positioning herself in between his legs so she could get close enough to adhere the bandage on both the front of his shoulder and the back.

He didn't answer her, merely shrugged as she smoothed the bandage over the slow-to-heal gunshot wound. His skin was surprisingly soft there, her hand looking particularly dark against the expanse of pale skin that rarely saw the sun.

Brady wasn't a shirtless guy, so his shoulder was all white marble, aside from the bandage she'd adhered herself.

She was standing between his legs and something…took over. It wasn't wanting to poke at him; it wasn't even that flare of attraction. This was something softer and different than she was used to and she didn't know how to fight off the urge to run her fingers through his hair.

He looked up at her, something flickering in his stoic gaze. It wasn't anger like usual. Or even annoyance at her. There was something deeper there. Her heart twisted and she suddenly wanted…

She wasn't sure. Not to throw herself at him or annoy him or try to start a fight. She didn't even want to act on that flare of attraction. She wanted… she didn't know. Just that it was deeper. Like he'd be some kind of salve to a wound.

"I get it. This is scary. You're scared for Mak," he said, his voice grave. Weighted, like he really did understand. "You're worried about your friend. It'd be nice to just chuck it all out the window for an hour or so. But it would change things. Things we can't afford to let change. It *would* mean something, whether either of us wanted it to."

She stared at him. He was right. It was terrible and true, and so completely right. And there was this part of her she didn't recognize that, for one second, wanted that change.

"Cecilia."

"Shh."

She cupped his face with her hands, and she ignored…everything she usually listened to. She did something without purpose, without certainty. She pressed her mouth to his, and it was almost timid. Not like she had on New Year's Eve—bold and a little drunk and mostly just *determined*. This was born of something else altogether. Seeking out that solace, or an understanding, that had always evaded her.

No one understood her. Not really. Not her family, not her friends, certainly not any ex-boyfriends. They thought she was tough and fearless.

But Brady had said she was scared for Mak, and she'd be damned if that wasn't the truth.

So, she kissed him with a softness she'd never found inside of herself.

He kissed her back. Not in that second of shock and reaction, but actual response. As if it was her gentleness that unlocked all his concerns and denials. And though she was standing, holding his face, there was no doubt that he took control of the kiss.

Kept it soft, kept it warm. Kept it like a connection, like a comfort.

She felt vulnerable, like her heart was soft. Like he wasn't just right, but had only scratched the surface when he'd said things would change.

It was fine enough to be attracted to Brady, to think sleeping with him would just solve that. It was something else for her to feel...*this* big thing.

She dropped her hands from his face and took two big steps back and away. "You're right. This is a bad idea. I'll stop." She had to gulp in some air to calm her shaky limbs, her even shakier heart.

He looked at her and the gaze was inscrutable. His words had no inflection whatsoever. "Well. Good, then."

The stoic way he delivered those words stung, even if they shouldn't. She was reeling—turned inside out, and he was a robot. "Fantastic."

And it was. She wasn't going to get *involved* with Brady Wyatt. After that kiss...she was willing to finally admit that if they acted on anything, involved was just what they'd be.

There was no way that was ever going to work. Not knowing that she'd sacrifice everything to keep Mak away from Elijah.

No, she had to listen to Brady for once and let this whole thing go. Because sliding in headfirst was a disaster waiting to happen.

Chapter Eleven

Even when it was his turn to sleep, Brady didn't do a very good job of it. Between the musty smell of the bed, the slightly sticky feel of the sheets, and the whirr of the pitiful air conditioner, there just wasn't much in the way of comfort.

Then there was his own…state. After Cecilia had kissed him on New Year's Eve, and even after yesterday morning with the truck, he'd been able to redirect the pang of attraction into indignant anger. A righteous certainty that she was wrong and he was in the right.

After last night's kiss, full of gentleness and something bigger than even he'd imagined, he didn't have that anger. Didn't have much of anything except confusion. And a baffling sense of loss.

Which didn't make any sense whatsoever, so he pushed the feeling and the nagging ache away and focused on the task at hand. It was always how he got through life. Why should this be any different?

They moved to the next motel on the west side of the county with limited conversation and absolutely no interference. Another night in another crappy motel with no one finding them passed in the same uncomfortable, grimy way. Another check-in with the Wyatt and Knight ranches to find nothing had really happened.

"I don't like it," Cecilia muttered, driving the truck north to another seedy motel in the neighboring county. They'd agreed she would drive when it was her turn to check into the motel and vice versa. "It shouldn't take this long to peg one of us. And the fact they're not going after the ranches… Something isn't right."

"If he's really been watching Ace, taking hints from Ace, he knows patience is Ace's greatest strength. Regardless, if they're not poking at the ranch, Mak is safe."

Cecilia slid him a look before returning her gaze to the road. "What do you know about Elijah that you haven't told me?"

"Nothing." If only because *know* was a tricky word when it came to Elijah Jones. He kept his expression carefully blank, ignored the need to shift in discomfort.

"I don't think that's true."

Brady shrugged and didn't elaborate. Cecilia kept driving.

The tension between them wasn't gone, but it had certainly shifted. Before it had been almost antagonistic and definitely argumentative. This was flat and…almost timid. Like they were suddenly tiptoe-ing around a bomb that might detonate.

He supposed, in a way, they were.

When Cecilia reached Frisco, a tiny town north of Valiant County, she did what they'd been doing this whole time. Found a deserted place to park the truck a block or so from the motel. In this case it was a roadside park surrounded by trees.

But she didn't immediately slide out of the truck to start her trek to the motel. She turned in the seat to face him, her expression grave.

"I need you to tell me whatever you know or think you might know. You keeping secrets about Elijah doesn't do anyone any good."

"I don't know anything, Cecilia. Anything I could say would be…supposition. Inference. Not fact."

Her eyebrows drew together. "I want those things from you. I think we need it all out in the open. I've told you everything I know about his relationship with Layla. Every time I've had an interaction with him on the rez or heard someone else relate one. You know my side. You're here, and I don't know your side. Just that you arrested him a long time ago and he's 'poked' at you ever since."

She wasn't wrong, much as he hated to admit it. Fact of the matter was, when Elijah was poking at him but never bothering his brothers, it didn't mat-ter. But that wasn't going to last, and if he'd kept this secret…

He didn't want it out in the open. Was always waiting for his worst fears to be disproven. But maybe he had played into Ace's hands the whole time.

He could ease into it. Lead Cecilia to her own conclusions, but because it was Cecilia, he knew he could just…blurt it out. She'd take it, work through it, and make her own opinion. He didn't have to lead her anywhere.

Still, the words stuck in his throat. He'd never vocalized his worst thoughts. Never wanted to. But he needed to do it—to keep Mak, and Cecilia, safe as he could.

She reached forward, rested her hand on his knee. Everything about her was earnest and almost… pleading. Which wasn't Cecilia at all.

The words tumbled out. "I think Ace might be Elijah's father."

"What?" Cecilia screeched. "How? Why? When? What?"

"Which of those questions do you actually want me to answer?" he replied dryly.

"Brady. Holy… Oh my God. Why do you think that?"

"I don't know," he returned, frustrated with things he couldn't fully name. "There's something about…" She was right, he reminded himself again. Knowing everything gave them ammunition. It gave them armor. Ace had made a habit of keeping secrets and using them against people.

Brady wouldn't be like his father. Wouldn't let

this potential secret, no matter how far-fetched, be the thing that felled him or Cecilia.

That didn't make it easy to explain the gut feeling he had. "Maybe he's not. But there's more to their relationship than a random Sons member taking a shine to our psycho in chief. Elijah would say things, when he'd goad me into arresting him. 'We're more alike than you think.' Lots of pointed remarks about my brothers. It just started to make me think…there's more there. Maybe it's not a father-son relationship, but there's more there. I can't imagine a man like Ace was faithful to my mother, especially toward the end when she was just getting pregnant to keep him from killing her."

"Did he kill her?" Cecilia asked, and her tone was simple. Straightforward. There wasn't that layer of pity he was so used to.

Which made it impossible to avoid, even if he hated this line of conversation. "Can't prove it."

"But you think he did," she insisted in that same even tone.

Brady shrugged jerkily. "Thinking it doesn't matter. Not when it comes to Ace and the Sons. Elijah being one of Ace's. We need fact."

Cecilia was quiet for a few humming moments. "I don't know about that," she said after a while. "If Elijah was Ace's son, don't you think we'd know?"

"Why would we?"

"Elijah wouldn't keep that a secret. He'd want everyone to know he was the president's son. He would have already taken over, I'd think."

"Unless Ace wanted him to keep it a secret." Brady shifted in his seat, wishing he'd kept his big mouth shut. "Like I said, Ace's best weapon is his ability to be patient. If he wanted to use Elijah when it would do the most damage… I'm just saying, there's a reason to keep it quiet. And it makes sense why he only ever hinted at the truth with me—why he focused on me. If he'd messed with all my brothers, wouldn't we put it together? But just one of us he could goad without the clues lining up."

"He's lived on the rez as long as I can remember."

It was suddenly too much. This was why he'd never brought it up with his brothers. It didn't matter when there was no way to know for sure. When it probably *wasn't* true. "I don't want to argue the validity, Cecilia. I'm just saying, that's my theory. One I don't even fully believe but you convinced me to tell you."

"You don't have to get touchy." She frowned out the windshield in front of them. "I'm trying to work it out. He's always lived on the rez, but he bounces from house to house. I don't know who his parents are. Not even his mother. I always figured they were both dead."

"And they very well might be."

"But your theory is based on eight years of watching this guy, right? Eight years of him toying with you. Eight years of you not telling anybody someone was harassing you." She blinked, looking up at him. "That's why you didn't tell your brothers."

He refused to meet her gaze. "I didn't tell them for lots of reasons."

"You didn't want them to have to think there were more Wyatts out in the world. Ones who didn't get out."

"Look. We're here." He pointed in the direction of where the motel would be. "Go check in and—"

"You could never be like them, Brady," she said quietly, but with a vehemence that had him looking over at her. "Jamison or no," she said, dark eyes straightforward and fierce. "Grandma Pauline or no. You could never be like them."

Something inside of him cracked, because it was the lie he'd always wanted to believe. But how could he? "We don't know that. I don't need to know that. Because I'm *not* like Ace or Elijah. But Ace and Elijah are the constant threats in my life, and I'm tired. I want this over. So, why don't you go check in, huh?"

She pursed her lips, but nodded eventually. "All right," she said, and slid out of the driver's side, leaving him in the truck alone with his thoughts.

Not a place he really wanted to be.

CECILIA'S MIND REELED as she walked toward the motel. Elijah as Ace's secret son. It made a creepy kind of sense. An awful kind of sense.

No matter how she tried to reason and rationalize it away, she kept coming back to the simple fact it was *possible*. Maybe even *probable*.

It put Mak in even more danger, especially with the Wyatts. Hell, it made Mak part Wyatt.

If it were true. She understood Brady's hesitation to believe it. There wasn't evidence and it didn't make sense why Ace would have kept it a secret. It also opened the horrible Pandora's box that Ace might have more children. Children who hadn't been saved like the Wyatt brothers had been.

And if Ace had kept them all a hidden secret— or even just Elijah—the reasons could only be bad. Really, really bad.

Cecilia stepped into the motel's cramped front office.

"Got a room available?" she asked the woman behind the counter, remembering belatedly to smile casually rather than frown over the problem in her head.

The woman looked her up and down.

"You a cop?"

Cecilia managed a laugh even as she inwardly chastised herself for walking in here with her cop face on. "No. I really look like one of those nosy bastards?"

The woman wasn't amused. "Got any ID?" she demanded with narrowed eyes.

"Oh, sure," Cecilia said casually even though her heartbeat was starting to pick up. The woman's careful inspection might just be the sign of a conscientious business owner.

But Cecilia doubted it.

She patted down her pockets. "Must have forgotten it in my car."

"Then I suggest you go get it, if you're really wanting to stay here."

Cecilia rolled her eyes. "My money ain't good enough for you, that's fine." She tried to sound flippant rather than irritated.

The woman behind the counter didn't say anything, just crossed her arms over her chest. Which Cecilia took as a clear sign that she would *not* be handing over any keys, regardless of money, without ID.

A little prickle of unease moved up the back of Cecilia's neck. She couldn't help but wonder if Elijah, or his men, had already been here and warned the woman off letting Cecilia get a room. She hadn't run into any motel owner this discerning yet.

Or maybe they'd been asking questions and that had simply made the woman nervous enough to take precautions.

The woman hadn't seemed afraid, though. Suspicious, distrusting and a little rude, yeah. But not afraid.

Cecilia moved back out of the office into the early-afternoon sun. She immediately picked out two men pretending to be otherwise occupied, but she knew they weren't. She didn't recognize them on a personal level, but she'd bet money they were Elijah's messengers.

She could take two. Unfortunately she had the sneaking suspicion there were more. Surely Elijah realized that she had no problem fighting off two of his pea-brained followers.

Still, she walked through the parking lot as if she didn't have a care in the world. She didn't have to look behind her to know the two were following her. Carefully and at a distance, but the farther she got from the hotel, the closer they got—to each other, and to her.

She'd made it maybe half a block, the park still not in view, when a man stepped out from behind a building in front of her.

Two behind. One in front. Not great odds, but if these three were as dim-witted as the two who'd knocked her off the road with Rachel, she could do it. Probably get a little banged up in the process, but she could do it.

She reached into her pocket and palmed her phone. She'd made a deal with Brady that if she didn't text within twenty minutes, he could come barreling after her. It hadn't been more than ten. Maybe she could get off a quick text and—

"Wouldn't do that if I were you." A fourth one popped out right next to her. Unlike the other three, who were likely armed but had their guns hidden, this one had his out and pointed at her. She froze with her hand still in her pocket.

As a police officer, Cecilia had learned how to defuse situations. How to talk men out of doing stupid things. Her goal, always, was to remain calm and use her words first.

As a woman in the world, she knew the opposite to be true. So, she didn't use her words, or wait.

She fought. Her immediate goal was disarming the man closest to her. She managed to get the gun out of his hand, but the others were quickly circling her.

She couldn't pay much attention to them when the one she'd disarmed was coming at her with a big, solid fist, but the fact no gunshots rang out meant they were supposed to keep her alive.

She had to hope.

She dodged the fist, landed a knee and her attacker dropped. She whirled to the ones she could feel closing in on her. They stood in a triangle around her. One had rope, one had a knife, and the other was just big as a Mack truck.

Crap.

Chapter Twelve

Brady surveyed the White River in the distance. It was narrow, the banks a grassy green where most of the landscape around him had gone brown under the heat of late summer. But here, near the river with a constant supply of life-giving water, things were green.

He tried to focus on that, on the landscape of his home state, on anything except the ticking seconds.

He'd promised Cecilia he wouldn't come barreling in like he had last time, though he did not characterize his previous actions as *barreling*. Still, there was no need today. They had their routine down pat and they'd found a compromise with her texting an okay after twenty minutes.

Still, the seconds seemed to tick especially slowly as he waited for a text message.

Brady got out of the truck. Not to *barrel* after her. Simply to stretch his legs. To walk off a little of his anxiety over the situation. Just in the little park.

He checked his watch. Twelve minutes down.

Now, *technically*, if it was twenty minutes from when they'd *stopped*, there'd only be three minutes left. And it would take him those three minutes to walk to the motel, so really he could head that way and not be breaking their deal.

She'd argue, but he had a…thin, shaky argument. Still, it *was* an argument.

She'd probably call it sexist, but he considered it just two different temperaments. She apparently couldn't fathom every possible worst-case scenario while she'd waited for him yesterday.

It was *all* Brady could think about while waiting for her. It wasn't a gender thing. It was a personality thing.

He'd start walking, but he'd do it slowly. Eke out the minutes but at least get the motel in his sights. Scout out a back way to get to the room without being detected.

Nothing wrong with that.

He locked the truck and started out. He stopped and frowned at a strange, faint noise. Something like a shout. Probably his imagination.

But maybe it wasn't, and he was a cop, trained to investigate that which didn't add up.

He moved stealthily up the street, hand already resting on his weapon with the holster unsnapped. He heard the noise again, closer this time, in the direct path between the park and the motel.

He forced away all those worst-case scenarios and focused on the task at hand. He approached the corner where he'd have to turn to continue the route to the motel. He took one calming breath, readied his body and his nerves, and then moved carefully to get a view of what was happening.

Immediately he could tell there was a fight. Four men—one on the ground crawling away from three men who seemed huddled around something. Maybe another person, it was hard to tell from this vantage point.

Brady inched forward, gun pointed in the direction of the scuffle. If he announced himself, they'd no doubt scatter and he wanted to get an idea of what was going on and descriptions of who he was dealing with before he decided which one to target.

The crawler wasn't going to be hard to pin down, but Brady noticed he was moving toward a small pistol. If he ran, he could beat the injured man to it, but judging by the fact he was hurt, the guy might just as well be a victim in the whole thing.

Brady glanced back at the trio. One let out a howl of pain and bent over, giving Brady a glimpse of what the three were huddled around.

He froze for less than a second, then immediately pointed his gun at the man crawling. No one had seen him yet, and shooting would put all four men on alert, but Brady couldn't let the crawling man get the gun. Not with Cecilia in the middle of that pack of jackals.

Brady shot, aiming for the arm that was reaching for the gun. The crawling man rolled onto his back, grabbing at his arm as he screamed. The three men around Cecilia jumped. They looked toward the crawling man, then wildly around until they found Brady.

Cecilia struggled to her feet, a piece of rope dangling from one arm, blood trickling down her face in a disturbing number of places.

Despite the fact she was clearly severely hurt, she didn't even pause. She kicked out, landing a blow to one's back. He stumbled forward, then whirled on Cecilia.

Brady charged forward as one man brandished a knife. Brady found it odd none of these three seemed to have guns, but he didn't have time to question it.

He ducked the first jab, pivoted and landed an uppercut so the man went pitching backward. Someone behind him landed a nasty kidney punch, but Brady only sucked in a breath and flung a fist backward. He connected with something that let out a sickening crunch followed by a wail of pain.

The knife flashed into his vision, and an ungainly leap backward allowed him to duck away from the sharp blade's descent with only a centimeter to spare. As the knife missed and momentum brought the assailant downward, Brady used his elbow as hard as he could.

A loud, echoing crack and the sound of a gurgling scream as the man stumbled onto his hands and knees. Brady kicked him with enough force to have the man falling onto his back. Brady stepped on his wrist—eliciting another gurgling scream from the man, but he let go of the knife.

Brady kicked it away and turned to find Cecilia. She'd taken one of the other men out, but the third man was trying to drag her by a rope he'd apparently tied around one of her arms.

"No, I don't think so," Brady said, reaching out and grabbing the taut rope. He ripped it out of the other man's grip with one forceful tug. He aimed his gun at the man's chest. "You want me to kill you, or you want me to let Elijah do it, nice and painful?"

The man sneered. "One of these days, every last high-and-mighty Wyatt's going to be wiped off this earth."

"I wouldn't count on it." Brady decided not to shoot—with the men unarmed he could call up the sheriff's department and have these four rounded up once he got Cecilia to safety. So, instead, Brady leapt forward and used the butt of the weapon to deliver a punishing blow to the head.

The man crumpled immediately and fell to the ground.

Brady whirled to Cecilia. She was kneeling next to the two men on the ground and had used the rope that had been tied around her wrist to tie them together.

"Want to add him?" she asked, her voice raspy. She was shaking, but she'd managed decent knots.

"He'll be unconscious for a while."

She struggled to get to her feet. There was blood just…everywhere. Parts of her shirt were torn and her hair had come completely undone so it was a wild tangle of midnight around her face.

"Almost had 'em," she managed to say before she swayed a little.

Brady scooped her up before she fell over. He didn't think he could stand to listen to her tell a bad joke in that ragged voice.

She wriggled slightly in his grasp as he started walking purposefully back to the truck. They weren't staying here. Not in this town or at that motel. He needed somewhere clean and sanitary to check out her wounds.

"I can walk."

"I can't say I care what you *can* do right now, Cecilia." He walked toward the crawling man who'd apparently gotten over the initial shock of his gunshot wound and was dragging himself toward the gun again.

"Don't know when to stop, do you?" Brady adjusted Cecilia's weight in his arms and then kicked the gun as hard as he could into the grassy field. If the injured man found the gun before Brady managed to call for backup, Brady'd consider him a magician.

He walked briskly back to the truck. With care, he placed Cecilia on her feet, though he kept one arm around her and supported almost all her weight.

"I'm fine," she muttered as he dug his keys out of his pocket. He ignored her and unlocked the truck, opened the door, then lifted her into her seat over her protestations. He even buckled the seat belt for her, though she weakly tried to bat his hands away. Then he looked her right in the eyes. "Don't you dare move," he ordered.

He was more than a little concerned that she listened.

CECILIA ONLY HALF listened as Brady drove and made a phone call. First she knew he was talking to the police. He was giving descriptions and accounts and locations of the fight that had transpired.

Cecilia closed her eyes against a wave of nausea. Four against one wasn't such great odds and as much as she'd held her own she was pretty banged up. She'd never admit it to Brady because he'd fuss, but she wasn't sure when she'd ever had such a bad beating.

But all four men would wind up in jail, and she would heal. So. There was that.

Brady made another call, driving too fast down deserted highways. She couldn't watch or she'd throw up. At first she'd figured he was calling his brothers, or worse, a hospital. But then he'd said something about cabins and fishing and her brain was a little fuzzy.

It was hard to focus and think over the bright fire of pain in various parts of her body. Harder still not to whimper every time the truck hit a bump. But if she showed any outward signs of pain Brady was going to baby her even worse than carrying her around.

It had been kind of nice to be carried but it was

certainly not behavior she wanted to encourage. Maybe it was the worst beating she'd ever gotten, but she'd been in her share of fights. Breaking them up, having big men take swings at her. She wasn't some helpless stranger to a few punches.

Of course, she'd never been stabbed before, and she wasn't quite sure how she was going to hide that from Brady. Surely she could find some Band-Aids and take care of it.

She winced a little, knowing it was probably too deep to be handled by a Band-Aid. It was fine, though. She'd figure it out. Brady would whisk her away to a hospital if he knew and that just couldn't happen. Not now when they'd delivered a blow to Elijah.

God, he'd be pissed she'd taken on *four* of his men. It almost made her smile to think of.

She wasn't sure if she'd fallen asleep or lost consciousness or what, but suddenly the truck was stopped and Brady was already standing outside. She tried to push herself up a little in her seat, but it nearly caused her to moan in pain.

She bit it back last minute as Brady was opening the passenger door.

"Where are we?" she demanded. She looked around, but nothing was familiar. They were on a little gravel lot and there was a scrubby little yard in front of a tiny, *tiny* cabin on a small swell of land.

Beyond the cabin was pure beauty. A sparkling lake stretching out far and wide, bracketed in by rolling rock. If she had to guess, they were closer to the Badlands than they'd been out in Valiant County.

It distracted her enough that Brady had her unbuckled and back in his arms before she had a chance to protest.

"I can walk, Brady."

"But you're not going to. Not until I check you out." He started walking, as if she weighed next to nothing and his shoulder hadn't been hurt for months. He took the little stone stairs up to the cabin without even an extra huff of breath.

"Buddy of mine's," he offered conversationally, even though his expression was completely... She didn't have a word for it. Tense, determined, fierce. "Well, more Gage's buddy. Pretended like I was Gage. Haven't done that since middle school, and it was never me. Gage was always the one pretending."

"He couldn't have fooled anyone who actually knew you two."

"You'd be surprised." He set her down, with the kind of gentle care one might use with a one-hundred-year-old woman. Then he futzed around with a planter in the shape of a bass. Something wilted and brown was growing out of the fish's mouth, but Brady pulled a key out from underneath.

He unlocked the door, pushed it open, then turned to her.

She held up her hands to ward him off. "If you pick me up again, I'm going to deck you."

With quick efficiency, he moved her hands away

and swept her into his arms again. Why did her stomach have to do flips every time he did that? And why couldn't she muster up the energy to actually punch him?

"Guess you're going to have to deck me."

She was so outraged she couldn't do anything but squeak as he marched her to the back of the cabin in maybe ten strides. He went straight into the bathroom and gently placed her on the floor again.

"Take off your clothes."

For a full ten seconds she could only stare at him. "I most certainly will *not*."

"You're bleeding God knows where. We need to get you cleaned up and patched up. Now. Shirt and pants off. You can leave your underwear on if you want to be weird about it, but I've got to see what kind of injuries we're dealing with."

"Weird ab—" She could feel fury and frustration somewhere deep underneath the pulsating pain of her body, but she couldn't seem to change any of that irritation into action. She leaned against the wall, trying to make it look like she was being casual, not needing something to prop her up. "Not the time to try to talk me into bed, Brady."

"Don't mess with me right now. Take off the clothes. I'm an EMT. I've seen plenty of naked women and manage to control myself each and every time. I have to see what kind of injuries you have so I know how to patch you up. Lose the clothes, Mills."

"How about you listen to the woman with the

injuries. I'm fine. Just a bit banged up. I'll take a shower—alone, thank you very much. If I need a bandage, I'll ask for your expert services."

It didn't have the desired effect—which was to get him to back off. She figured it might at least hurt his pride a little if she took a shot at the EMT side of his profession. She knew Brady took the paramedic stuff very seriously, that he'd once wanted to be a doctor. Acting like all he did was slap on bandages should offend him.

But he merely narrowed his eyes at her. "What are you trying to hide?"

She bristled, her tone going up an octave. "Nothing."

"Bull," he returned. "You want to be difficult? Fine. I'll do it myself."

He moved toward her, and if she'd been 100 percent she would have fought him off. She would have done whatever it took to keep his hands off her.

But she was beaten up pretty good. There wasn't any fight left in her, there was only fear, and she was very afraid she'd cry if she let him take her shirt off her.

So, she whipped it off herself. It wasn't about being shirtless in front of him. Her sports bra was hardly different than a swimsuit or what she'd wear to the gym. But she knew his reaction to her wounds was going to…hurt somehow.

He swore, already leaping for the little cabinet under the sink. In possibly five seconds flat he had a washcloth pressed to the stab wound. She hadn't dared look at it herself, but maybe she should have, judging by the utter fury in his gaze.

"What the hell were you thinking?"

"It's not that bad," she said weakly. Maybe it was bad enough to have mentioned it. She'd only wanted to handle it herself. She didn't need him manhandling her and…

She blinked, desperately holding on to the tears that threatened. She didn't want to break down in front of him ever again. That one time in his apartment over Mak was bad enough. This would be worse.

Because she wasn't sad or upset. It was the adrenaline of the fight wearing off. It was the need for release. She didn't want to be petted or taken care of.

She wanted to be alone. To handle it herself. To build all her defenses back without someone here… taking care of her. Because if he took care of her, he'd see all the marks of how she'd failed to take care of herself.

What kind of cop was she, then?

She looked up at the ceiling, didn't answer his questions and definitely didn't dare look at him. She blinked and blinked and focused on staving off the tide of tears.

But then he did the damnedest thing. He rested his forehead on her shoulder and let out a shuddering breath. Something deep inside of her softened, warmed, fluttered. Without fully thinking through the move, she lifted her arm that didn't hurt too much and rested her hand on his head.

"I'm okay. Really," she managed to say without sounding as shaky as she felt. "Just a little flesh wound."

The sound he made was some mix of a groan of frustration and a laugh.

"You've fixed worse on people," she reminded him. "Your own brothers in fact."

He shook his head, but lifted it from her shoulder. He didn't look at her, his gaze was on the washcloth he was pressing to the wound. "All right." He blew out another shaky breath, but the inhale was steadier. He seemed to shrug off the moment. When his eyes finally met hers, they were clear, steady and calm. "Let's get you really cleaned up, and I'll see what I can do for the stab wound."

Chapter Thirteen

Brady instructed Cecilia to hold the towel firm against her wound. Even the brief glimpse he'd gotten told him she needed stitches. He was no stranger to stitching up his brothers, but mostly as a paramedic that skill was left to doctors at the hospital.

He started the shower and tried to focus on the practicalities. She didn't just have the stab wound. She had bruises and he'd need to make sure she hadn't broken anything. He'd also need to check for a head wound because she'd dozed off in the truck—whether exhaustion as the adrenaline wore off or loss of consciousness he couldn't be sure until he examined her.

But first and foremost she had to get the grime and blood off of her. She could stand and she was lucid, so a quick shower was the best option.

The fact she hadn't even acted like she was in that much pain just about did him in. Why had she hidden it? To what purpose?

He couldn't focus on that. He'd nearly fallen apart

when she'd finally taken off her shirt and he'd seen that deep, bloody gash.

It hadn't even occurred to him she was *that* hurt. She'd been acting so…flippant. At least when he'd worked on his brothers it had always been pretty visible how bad off they were up front. And when he dealt with them he'd have privacy after to rebuild his defenses.

There wasn't going to be any privacy here until the Elijah threat was taken care of.

Still, he was a trained EMT. He should have a better handle on his reactions and he would. He would.

"Do you think you can handle a shower?"

"No. Why don't you sponge bathe me, Brady? Of course I can handle a *shower*. You know, if you give me some privacy."

"Sorry. I'm not going anywhere until we know you didn't suffer a head injury."

"I didn't."

"How do you know?"

"Wouldn't I know if I got knocked in the head?"

He didn't look at her, even to give her a raised-eyebrow look. "Does your head hurt?"

She was stubbornly silent, which was as clear a *yes* as an immediate denial would have been.

"I'll keep my eyes closed." He moved away from the shower that was going, nice and hot, enough to make the room a little hazy.

"You don't have to be *that* much of a gentleman. I

don't think a glimpse of nipple is going to send you into a crazed sex haze."

Still, Brady kept his back to her and the shower. "Use soap," he instructed, trying to pretend like she was a child who needed to be told what to do. Not someone some warped part of his brain wanted to see naked.

Which could *not* be considered, so he focused on the next. He had a first aid kit in his pack. It had the appropriate disinfectant. He didn't have anything strong enough to numb the area where she'd need to get stitches. That was going to be a problem, because while he was in no doubt she'd handle it, he wasn't so sure *he* could handle giving her that much pain.

"Probably gonna need a little help with the sports bra," she said after a few seconds. "It clasps in the back, but…"

She didn't come out and say one of her arms hurt, but that was clearly the implication. She couldn't get them both behind her back, which was a bad sign. "You have to be in a lot of pain," he said flatly, turning to face her.

She still held the cloth to the gash on her side. "I'm alive, Brady. Managed to hold off four guys, one with a knife and one with a gun. I'll take the pain, thanks." She frowned. "What pack of four morons only brings one gun to kidnap someone?"

"The kind that aren't allowed to kill you," Brady said wryly, motioning for her to turn around so he could unclasp her bra for her. "Elijah will want to hurt you himself. Trust me. It's why my brothers and I are still alive." He focused on that, not the smooth expanse of her back.

She shivered—he was sure because of what he was saying, not because his fingers brushed her bare back to unclasp the bra.

"So, why doesn't he come after us?"

Brady forced himself to drop his hands and turn around again. "That I haven't quite figured out. Do you need help with anything else?"

"No. I think I can manage."

Brady focused on finding a towel rather than the sound of her taking off her pants or stepping into the shower. He breathed in the heavy, steamy air and refused to think about showers or nakedness, because the naked woman was hurt and bleeding with a potential head injury. He wouldn't even be able to determine if she had breaks or fractures. He wasn't a doctor. He didn't have the right equipment.

He should take her to a hospital. It left them with less control of the situation, but she'd get checked out. Fully checked out. It had to be worth the risk.

The water stopped and Brady heard the clang of the curtain rings moving against the shower curtain rod.

He held out the towel, keeping his gaze and body angled away from her.

The towel was tugged from his hands. "God, do you have to be so noble?" she demanded irritably as if it were some flaw.

"I don't know how to respond to that."

"Of course not. I managed to stay upright in the shower. Are you going to let me walk on my own or do I get the princess treatment again?"

"Put pressure on that gash," he instructed, rather than answer her question. "We should—"

"If you mention the word *hospital* I won't be responsible for my reaction, Brady. You're a trained, licensed EMT. You can check me out."

"You need stitches."

"I'm fine."

"You're not. I can tell without even a full examination that it's deep, long and in a bad spot. We bend and move our sides far more than we know. If you don't get stitches, not only is it going to scar, but we're going to have to watch out for too much blood loss. Infection is a near certainty, and just plain not healing is an even bigger one."

"He says, from experience," she replied sarcastically.

She didn't know the half of it. "I know my way around a knife wound personally and medically, Cecilia."

"Get in a lot of knife fights?"

He ignored the question. Just closed that whole part of him off, encased it in ice. Had to or he'd never get through this.

"Oh, turn around for Pete's sake," she muttered. "I've got the towel on."

"A hospital would be a better bet," he insisted.

Though he did turn around and face her, he kept his gaze on her eyes. Refused to dip to even her nose. Didn't check the towel placement or if she was putting pressure on her side where the gash was.

"Surely it's not that bad."

He tried not to let his irritation, and all the other feelings clawing inside his chest, get the best of him. "It's not that good."

"Right, but you've patched up worse," she insisted.

"Yeah. Usually with help or better supplies. I had an actual medical doctor talk me through fixing up Cody after his car accident, and that was only until he could get to the hospital. I don't have what I'd need to stitch you up, and you need more than a temporary solution."

"I'll be fine with a temporary solution." She waved a careless hand. "Just do what you can."

It was that carelessness, the utter refusal to listen to him that had his temper snapping. Every time his brothers came to him and said the same thing. Years of that, the past few months especially. Everyone was so sure they were *invincible* simply because he knew some basic emergency medical treatment.

He sucked it up and did his best, knowing it might not be good enough. What else was there to do?

But she didn't seem to get it. She was *seriously* hurt, and he wasn't a damn magician. "Did it occur to you—any of you ever—that you might not be fine? That I'm *not* a doctor. That I can't just magically *fix*

you all when you come to me bloody and broken because of Ace Wyatt."

She stood very still, regarding him with a kind of
blankness in her expression he recognized because
it was the same face he put on when dealing with
someone not quite stable.

"This doesn't have to do with Ace," she said,
softly, almost sympathetically.

Which pissed him off even more. "It all has to do
with Ace. Always. And forever. Now I need to find
someplace to examine you, so stay put."

CECILIA WAS ALMOST tempted to do as Brady ordered
as he stormed out of the small bathroom. There'd
been something painful about his little outburst. A
little too much truth in his frustration. If she stayed
put, he'd compartmentalize it away and they could
focus on the real problems in front of them.

But the fact he had all of that… Insecurity wasn't
the right word. She was certain Brady understood his
abilities, and knew he was an excellent EMT. The
thing none of them had ever really thought about was
the fact that doctors and EMTs weren't supposed to
work on their families. That's when emotions came
into play, and that put undue stress on the people
doing the work.

The past few months, Brady had been tasked with
working on some of the people he loved most in the
world. They'd all asked it of him without a second
thought—because it had been necessary. But no one

seemed to think about the emotional toll it might put on the one cleaning up everyone else's injuries.

Especially while he was still trying to heal from his own complicated injury.

Cecilia inhaled. She didn't need to feel sorry for Brady. She was the one standing here wet, naked under a towel, bleeding and bruised. *She* was the one people should feel sorry for.

Trying to keep that in mind, she finally forced herself to move out of the bathroom and into the rest of the cabin. There was a kitchen/dining/living room all in the center, but right next door to the bathroom was another door.

It was open, and Brady was inside the bedroom fussing with the bedding. He'd already set out a line of first-aid stuff on one side of the bed. He didn't even look up, though clearly he knew she was standing there.

"Lay down. Once I've made sure everything aside from the stab wound is fine, you can get dressed and we'll decide what to do from there."

"No broken bones, Brady. No head wound. I've had both, I'd know what they'd feel like. I've got one nasty cut there, and a much less nasty one on my back. The rest are scratches that don't need any attention and bruises that could use some ibuprofen or some ice or a heating pad."

"Lay down, please."

She groaned at his overly solicitous tone, but she slid into the bed, still holding the towel around her.

Once she was settled, Brady pulled the blanket up to her waist, then carefully rolled the towel up to reveal her abdomen without showing off anything interesting. Didn't even try.

Seriously, would it kill the guy to try to cop a feel or something?

He'd put on rubber gloves and immediately began inspecting the stab wound on her side. He sighed and shook his head as he inspected it. "I know what happens to a wound this deep that doesn't get stitches, Cecilia. We need to get to a hospital."

"Let's say we don't—"

"Ce—"

"Hear me out. Let's say we give it another couple days. You wash it out, bandage it up, and we try to get a few answers on Elijah's whereabouts or plan. *Then* I go to the hospital and get it stitched up. What's the risk of a few days?"

"Infection," he said, so seriously as if that was going to scare her off.

"Last time I checked, they have meds for that. Which you should be well acquainted with."

"I'm also well acquainted with what happens when you try to let a wound like this heal on its own but don't actually take it easy."

"How?"

"How what?" he muttered irritably. He grabbed some disinfectant from his lineup of first aid and Cecilia immediately tensed, waiting for the pain.

"How are you well acquainted with what happens

when you don't care of a wound like this?" she asked through gritted teeth, waiting for the sting.

He stared at her for a full five seconds like she'd spoken in tongues, holding the cotton swab in one hand. "I...have a dangerous job." He focused back on her wound. "This is going to hurt."

She snorted. "Look, I'm a cop too. I know we get into dangerous situations and we get hurt. I'm sure we've both got a few scars from *work*. But getting stabbed isn't exactly a day at the office." She hissed the last word out as the disinfectant stung like fire. "I think I would have heard about your stab wounds."

After a few humming breaths as she tried not to outwardly react to the sting, Brady spoke. His words were quiet and measured, but there was something lingering inside of him that was neither. "What do you think happens when you're a kid in a gang, Cecilia? Someone bakes you brownies?"

She blinked. *Oh.* Well, of course. Being hurt and not getting medical attention was probably life in the Sons of the Badlands. She just so often forgot he'd actually...spent years there. Innocent, vulnerable years. He was so good. So strong. She couldn't even picture it knowing what he'd looked like as a boy—reserved and gangly. It *hurt* trying to imagine. "Who stabbed you? Other kids?"

He was silent, but he was unwrapping butterfly bandages from their plastic wrapper, which meant she was getting out of a mandatory hospital visit for now.

"Brady."

He paid very careful attention to the wound on her side as he attached the bandages, one by one, along the line of sliced skin. "Ace had a game, is all. A nice little game just for me. Usually he missed."

Cecilia's blood went cold, but she knew if she let that seep into her voice he'd shut down and shut her out. She breathed, steadied her voice. "Usually?"

He shrugged, attached another bandage.

Then it dawned on her. She'd seen him with his shirt off that first night. She'd been somewhat surprised he'd been so marked up, but it hadn't occurred to her to wonder *why.* "All those scars. They're from not-misses. He stabbed you."

"He threw knives," Brady corrected, as if that were better instead of somehow worse. "Gotta learn to expect the unexpected. Though he was always pulling them out to toss my way, so I'm not sure how it was unexpected, but here I am trying to rationalize a madman's thinking."

"He threw knives at you," Cecilia said, because she *couldn't* picture that. Not just because it caused her pain, because it was nonsensical. It was *insane.*

Brady lifted his gaze to hers over the bandages. She realized she'd let emotion, horror mostly, seep into her tone.

"I'm alive, Cecilia. I survived. But I'd rather not take a trip down memory lane if you don't mind. Can you sit up?"

She blinked. It was her turn to feel like a foreign

language was being spoken. After a few seconds she managed to sit up. He put a pad of gauze over the butterfly bandages, then used a wrap bandage around her waist to keep it in place.

"This is stupid. You need stitches. The chance of infection, of losing too much blood, of this not healing, are extraordinarily large."

She heard the exhaustion in his tone. The worry. And maybe even the ghost of a little boy whose father had thrown knives at him. She hadn't had that rough of a childhood. She'd thought it had been the worst, but it really hadn't been. Being poor and neglected and then moved into a loving house at the age of six had nothing on Brady's experience.

But she thought they needed the same thing in the face of those old ghosts. The only thing that had ever helped her had been to face down the current ones. And win. "Elijah's not coming for us, Brady. We have to go to him."

She thought he might pretend to misunderstand her, but his words were stark. "We don't know where he is."

"I know where he'll be. I know you do too."

Brady inhaled. "I promised myself a long time ago that I'd never go back there, Cecilia." He met her gaze. "Never."

She was closer to crying than she'd even been in the bathroom, but she didn't look away. "We need to."

Chapter Fourteen

Brady didn't precisely agree with Cecilia, but in the end he didn't argue with her. He'd patched her up best that he could, got her some clothes from her pack, ibuprofen for the pain, and ice for the particularly nasty bump under her eye—because apparently she'd gotten hit in the same exact spot as a few nights ago.

He ignored his own aches and pains as he ran through a shower. They'd agreed to spend the night at the cabin and get a fresh start in the morning. A fresh start doing *what* was still up in the air.

Go to the Sons camp? He'd promised himself he'd never do that, with one simple caveat: only if his brothers ever needed him to.

Cecilia wasn't his brother. Mak wasn't his brother. But wasn't it all the same? You went back if you had to protect the people you...cared about.

Brady dried off from the shower, examined his own injuries. His gunshot wound continued to heal, and that was something to be thankful for. He had a riot of bruises rising across his chest and arms, but that was to be expected after the fight they'd had. He was in a lot better shape than Cecilia.

He'd brought in a change of clothes but forgotten to grab his own stash of bandages. They were going to run out at the rate they were going.

He took a moment to look at himself in the foggy mirror. He wasn't sure what he'd expected when he'd started down this path. He hadn't really *planned*—he'd only wanted to protect.

He'd been somewhat…disapproving of his brothers rushing in to face what they'd all left behind. He'd understood Jamison's need to help Liza save her young half sister from the human trafficking ring the Sons had been starting. A person, especially Jamison, couldn't turn his back on that. And yes, Cody obviously had to save his ex and his secret daughter from Ace's threats. And when Gage helped investigate the murder Felicity had been framed for, of course it ended up connecting to the Sons.

Everything did.

He'd known going in Elijah had ties to the Sons and his father, so going back to Sons territory seemed inevitable.

Still, he recoiled from it.

He scrubbed his hands over his face. A good night's sleep and surely he'd have a better handle on everything roiling around inside of him. He'd be able to compartmentalize and function as he normally did.

But there was something about *this* situation that

made it harder. He'd patched up Cody's horrendous injuries. He'd helped Gage after he'd been basically tortured by Ace. Granted, those were after-the-fact situations. Mopping up a mess, not wading into one while worrying about the woman wading into it with him.

He didn't understand it, though. He trusted Cecilia, as much as any one of his brothers, to take care of herself. He didn't understand why this felt harder. Maybe it was his own weakness. A mental softening from all his time off.

He stepped out of the bathroom, determined to shove it all away again.

She was sitting up in the bed, though he'd told her to be as still as possible. Her hair was damp and leaving spots of wet on her T-shirt. She had an impressive bruise forming on her cheek.

She was not a weak woman, or even a soft one. She was all angles and muscle with a smart mouth and a sharp mind, who could take care of herself and save herself, no questions asked. He did not understand his desperate desire to wrap her up and keep her far from harm.

He wanted to protect his brothers, no doubt, and same for the Knight girls. He'd quickly and easily thrown himself in the way of harm to protect them, save them.

But this was different. This *thing* he felt toward Cecilia was different, and not liking it and pushing it away didn't seem to change anything.

When she glanced his way, she threw the covers off and started to move. "Oh my God, Brady. Look at you."

"Don't you dare get out of that bed. You are supposed to keep that cut immobile." He looked down at himself and frowned. "What?"

"You're *covered* in bruises," she said, outrage tingeing her words, though she had stopped herself from getting out of bed. "You didn't say you'd been hurt."

"I'm not hurt. Like you said, I know what serious injuries feel like. Just a little bruising."

"These aren't little. And there are quite a few."

"You really want to have this argument when I can still load you up in that truck and take you to a hospital?" He stalked over to his pack and pulled out the bandage and disinfectant he needed for his shoulder.

"You really *don't* want to have this argument when you gave me hell for not telling you right away I'd been stabbed?"

"Stabbed. A stab wound that needs stitches and I—"

"You're insufferable." She held out a hand toward him when he sat down on the opposite side of the bed. "Give it to me."

"You need to be still."

"Give me the damn bandage, and scoot over here if you don't want me to move."

He grumbled and did as he was told. She smoothed the bandage on the back side, then he turned so she could do the front as well.

She touched his most pronounced scar, which was in a similar spot as her wound. The injuries were in fact quite similar, though he'd been ten when he'd gotten his. She sighed. "I don't know how you survived this and still became you, Brady. I really don't."

He shrugged, trying to ignore the effect her touch had on him. "You just do." He reached for his shirt, but something about her touching his scar kept him from his full range of motion.

"*You* do. You did. I know you don't want to go back there." She looked up at him, though her fingers lingered on his scar. "I don't want you to have to go back there."

"If you're about to suggest you go alone, you can—"

"No. No, I know better than that, believe it or not. We have to do this together. Have each other's backs. At some point that might mean splitting up, but not yet."

"Not ever."

She studied his face, as if looking for something. An answer. A clue. A truth. She reached out and cupped his cheek with her hand, the other hand still pressed to his scar.

He held himself very still, trying to think back to all the arguments he'd had against this when she'd been throwing herself at him to irritate him.

But this wasn't that. Even he knew this wasn't that.

"Brady, I really thought I was going to die. Maybe

not out there, but if they'd gotten me, taken me to Elijah, I knew it was over."

Fury spurted through him. "He won't—"

"Shh," she said lightly, her thumb brushing against his cheekbone. "I'd do it. I don't *want* to, but if it would keep Mak safe, I'd die for him. I think we all feel that about our families, but I've never actually been put in a position where I had to specifically accept it would be at someone's hands. Elijah's hands."

Maybe she wouldn't let him say it, but he'd do everything in *his* power to make sure that never, *ever* happened.

"I don't want him to take anything from me. I will fight tooth and nail to make sure you and Mak *and* I come out of this in one piece. I'm not being fatalistic here, I'm just telling you…"

She cupped his other cheek, moved so they were knee to knee. He would have admonished her for moving, but her body brushed his—lightning and need.

"I know it would change everything, but maybe everything needs to change. Maybe it's already changed."

He had to clear his throat to speak. "It wouldn't just change us. Our families. Duke isn't exactly thrilled with my brothers for similar happenings."

Her smile was soft, her touch on his face even softer. "Duke doesn't approve of anything I've done. Becoming a cop. Living on the rez. Et cetera. He loves me anyway." She trailed her fingers over his cheeks. "You didn't have to do any of this. I brought you into this. I plopped Mak in your arms and—"

"Elijah already—"

"Shut up and *listen*, Brady. I came to you and convinced myself it was because you were the one who had the time, but it was because you were the one I trusted. I could have gone to Jamison or Cody— they have experience keeping children away from the Sons' reach. I could have gone to Tucker, he's a detective for heaven's sake. They all would have helped me. I came to you."

He didn't know how to react to that, or how to sift through the assault of emotions. Hope too big among them.

But then he didn't have to, because she kissed him. It was soft and gentle. He didn't think either of them had much of that in their lives. Maybe it was why they needed to show it to each other.

Maybe all this time he'd avoided her and that New Year's Eve kiss because he hadn't wanted to allow himself that. It certainly didn't feel right to take it now, except she needed it too.

And how could he resist giving her what she needed?

CECILIA WASN'T SURE what had changed inside of her. Only that something had opened up or eased. Something had shifted to make room for this, and once it had, she couldn't hide it away again.

She'd kissed Brady on New Year's Eve because

he made her feel something she couldn't name, and for a long time she hadn't wanted to. Still, it hadn't gone away so she'd convinced herself it was merely attraction and backed off when Brady made her understand it couldn't be only that.

Now, just a little while later, she was the one kissing him. Saying things had already changed.

His hands were gentle, his kiss was *dreamy*, and it was as if those tiny pieces inside of her that had still felt so out of place clicked together and made sense.

If it hadn't been for this afternoon, fear of change would have continued to win—continued to keep her hands off when it came to Brady. But fear of death—and the possibility of that death being very much right in her face—made the fear of change weaker. Change was hard, but regret was too steep a price to pay.

What would be the point of this life she'd been given if she didn't accept all the emotions inside of her? She wasn't perfect. She wasn't even good half the time, but the things she felt for Brady were real. They were here.

Why had she been avoiding that? To not be embarrassed? To not be hurt? It seemed so *silly* in the face of what could have been her last day on earth. Maybe that was dramatic, but it had led her here.

No one had ever kissed her like she was both fragile and elemental all at the same time. But it was more than just the kiss.

No man, including Duke—the only man in her

life she'd let herself truly love as both uncle and father figure—had ever made her feel understood. No one in her whole life had made it seem like the strong parts of her and the weaker parts of her were one complex package...one that someone could still want and care for. She was either fully strong or fully weak to others, but inside she was both.

She didn't want to be protected, but sometimes she wanted to be soothed. She didn't need anyone to fight her fights, but sometimes she needed someone to dress her wounds. Literally. Figuratively.

Brady was that. Just...by being him.

His fingers tightened in her hair, and the kiss that had begun as soft and lazy heated, sharpened. Something ignited deep inside of her, a hunger she hadn't really thought *could* exist inside of her. It had certainly never leapt to life before.

But now...now she wanted to sink into that heat and that unfurling desperation. It was new and it was heady and it was better than all that had come before.

But she could feel Brady pulling back. "You're hurt," Brady murmured against her mouth, as if he wanted to break the kiss but couldn't quite bring himself to.

She was vaguely aware of her sore body, but mostly those aches and pains were buried underneath the sparkling warmth of lust. She didn't just want a kiss, she wanted Brady's body on hers. She wanted to get lost for a few minutes in something other than pain and fear.

Some part of her she didn't fully understand wanted the hope of more with Brady when this was all over. Change seemed better than standing in the same place feeling alone. Feeling as though no one understood her or loved her as a whole, complex human being.

She sank into another kiss, desperate for him to forget her injuries. Forget where they were and what they had to do and finish *this*.

"I'll live," she insisted. "I want this, Brady. I want you."

He undressed her, and she *knew* he was being mindful of her injuries, but she didn't *feel* it. She felt worshipped and surrounded by something bigger than she could describe. A light, a warmth, a renewal of who she was.

Made somehow more awe-inspiring by the fact the man currently kissing her scrapes and caressing her many bruises was…gorgeous. He was all muscle and control. In another world he might have been a movie star, if he wasn't so raw and real. So… Brady. Good and noble and making her body hum with a desperate need she was sure, so *sure*, he could take care of.

And he did, entering her, moving with her, a gentle, heated tangle of all those things she'd been afraid of: change, need, hope.

Why had those been fears? When they were this *good*. This comforting and *right*.

He said her name and it echoed inside of her. It

felt like a hushed *finally*. Like they'd been waiting all their years to do this, when she didn't think they had. Certainly not consciously.

But it was here now, and she knew this was just… it. Him. Them.

She slid her fingers through his hair, focused on pleasure over the pain of her injuries, and gave herself over in a way she'd never done before. Because she trusted Brady. Wholeheartedly. He was the person she went to when she was in the most trouble, and he was the person she wanted to be with in this dangerous, desperate situation.

Always.

The crest of release washed over her, a slow roll of pleasure and hope and relaxation. A *finally* whispered through her body as Brady followed her into oblivion.

She sighed into his neck, snuggled in when he carefully tucked her against his body, and slept.

Chapter Fifteen

When Brady's phone trilled, waking him from a deep, restful sleep, he jerked, then immediately relaxed his body so he didn't jostle Cecilia, still curled up against him. Naked.

He hadn't meant to fall asleep. Then again he hadn't meant to sleep with Cecilia. But both had happened and left him feeling…settled. Instead of the scatterbrained panic, hopping from one problem to another, he felt clearheaded.

Guilt could seep in if he let it. That this was the wrong time and the wrong place and it was not precisely…*right.*

But it had felt right. Righter than most of the choices he'd made in the past year or so.

He had spent a lot of years in his life convincing himself that no one could understand him like his brothers did. They'd shared a kind of tragedy, something other people couldn't imagine. Based on the way Cecilia had reacted to his explanation of his scars, she couldn't imagine it either.

But she treated him like something other than the

boy who'd spent his formative years in that gang. More than a piece of the Wyatt whole.

He yawned when his phone trilled again. He'd almost forgotten that's what had woken him up in the first place. A repeated phone call when the world was still dark could mean nothing good. He grabbed his phone and saw Cody's name on the screen.

He only got half of his brother's name out before Cody was talking over him. "There's been a fire at Duke's. Everyone's safe and fine, but it was set purposefully and in the middle of the night like this. It was meant to scare us."

Any good feelings or relaxation seeped out of him. He tensed and disentangled himself from Cecilia, pushing into a seated position on the bed. "You're sure everyone's all right?"

"Thank God for Dev making the dogs stay with us at the Knights'. Cash was barking before I think the thing was even lit. I thought for sure it was a ploy to get us out, but nothing else happened. We're all over at Grandma's and we haven't been able to find anyone on the property."

"What is it?" Cecilia hissed from behind him.

He waved her off. "It's got to be Elijah, though."

"Seems the only option. Everyone is fine, so I'm not sure what his purpose was. They got around my security measures, but didn't actually hurt anyone or take Mak? All these near misses seem…unlikely."

"Yeah. Yeah, they do. Listen, I've got to explain it to Cecilia. Then we'll go from there. Keep watch, though. Be careful. Anything else happens, keep us updated."

"Same," Cody said before Brady ended the call.

"What is it?" Cecilia demanded, before he'd fully pressed End. "Mak? Is it—"

He took her hands in his, trying to find his own calm and reason before he attempted to give her any. "Mak is fine. Everyone is fine. There's been a fire at Duke's house. Luckily, Dev had been making Sarah take care of his dogs and they—"

She immediately threw the sheets off and began to pick up her clothes. He could tell she regretted the sudden movements by the hiss of her breath, but she kept going. "We have to go. We have to go to them."

"No. No, I don't think so." He got out of bed himself, slid his own boxers and shorts back on before crossing to her side of the bed where she was now fully dressed and looking at him furiously. "Sit down. Don't hurt yourself. Listen."

"Listen? Listen!" She waved her arms wildly, then winced. "They burn down Duke's house—his *house*—at night which means even if they're okay Duke and Sarah and oh, God, Brianna and Nina were staying there and Rachel, she—"

Brady stood in front of her and took her hands in his again. It was the only thing to keep her still, and when she tugged he squeezed hard enough to have her taking a sharp breath. "Another one," he ordered. "Deep breath in, and then out."

He didn't expect her to listen, but she did. Still,

when her gaze met his it was determined. Haunted.
"We have to go. Now."

"Cecilia, no. We can't do that. This is what he
wants from you. From us. Think."

She wrenched her hands out of his, groaning out
loud this time. "I don't give a flying leap what he
wants from me. He burns down my family's home
and thinks I'm going to what? What would you have
me do, Brady? Sit here? No. I refuse. I don't care
what Elijah's plans are."

"You need to," he said sharply. He didn't like
being sharp with her, not right now, so he softened
his words by cupping her face with his hands. "*We*
need to. Remember you're not alone. Mak's not alone.
So, we have to work through that fear and not let it
lead us. That's what he wants. It's what they always
want. When fear wins, so do they." He couldn't let
Elijah win *ever*, but now it seemed even more im-
perative to find an end. For all of them. So Cecilia
could heal, so Duke could rebuild, so they could
live…normally, if that was ever possible.

She rested her hands over his on her face. "But
I *am* afraid, Brady," she said in little more than a
whisper.

He knew that was a great big hard admission for
her, so he made his own. "I know. So am I. Fear is
normal. We just can't let it make the decisions. When
you got Mak, you didn't panic. You didn't run right
to me. You made plans. You were careful, and so far
Mak is safe and sound. So that's what we have to do."

She sucked in a breath and nodded with it. "Okay, okay. Maybe you're right. I knew… I knew I couldn't just run with him or he'd be hurt. I had to think. I had to plan. So, yeah. That's what we have to do. So… He set a fire—"

"That didn't hurt anyone. It's important to remember that. Everyone is fine. He set a fire to lure us home. To *scare* us home. I believe that. Don't you?"

She didn't answer right away. He could tell she gave herself the time and space to really think it over. "Yeah. He's tired of sending his goons after us and failing. He's setting a trap."

"We can't fall for it. We need to do the opposite of what he'll expect. I think…" He sighed heavily. This changed things. There was no escaping what he'd hoped to avoid. "You were right. We need to go into Sons territory. He doesn't think we will, which means we'll have the element of surprise. We need to take him off guard. It's the only way we win."

She searched his face, as if looking for doubt or that earlier reticence. She didn't find it. He wouldn't let her.

She nodded once. "All right. Let's pack."

BRADY EXPLAINED TO her where the fishing cabin was located, and that it wasn't that far from the Sons' current camp on the east side of the Badlands. They were going to have to be strategic about where and how they entered the area, but getting there wouldn't be too long of a haul.

They'd both gotten a couple hours sleep, and that would have to tide them over for a while. She wanted to be in Sons territory by sunrise, but they'd have to hurry.

She didn't let herself think about Mak, or her childhood home being on fire. She didn't think of poor Nina and Cody having to get Brianna out, or what the confusion might have done to Rachel in worse circumstances. She couldn't even begin to let herself think about what would have happened if the dogs hadn't been there.

Her brain wanted to go in *all* those directions, but she couldn't let it. She had to focus on Elijah. How to take him off guard. How to take him down before he did another thing to hurt or scare her family.

"I found a backpack," Cecilia offered, coming into the bedroom where Brady was carefully counting first aid items and foodstuffs and the few camping supplies Grandma Pauline had thought to pack them. "We can both carry a pack now," Cecilia said.

"You better fill yours with bandages and anything that can be used as bandages," Brady muttered.

"I think we've got a lot bigger fish to fry than fussing over a few…" She trailed off at the look he gave her. It was a warning and a censure and yeah, a little hot. Since they didn't have time for a repeat earlier performance she held up her hand. "Okay, the injuries are dangerous and we have to take them seriously."

"You shouldn't be hiking, camping or fighting off

biker gang members at all. Nothing is going to heal. *Something* will get infected, and I promise you it's not the picnic you seem to think."

"I suppose not, but once we do all those things, and get Elijah arrested, you can lock me up and nurse me back to health in whatever ways you see fit."

He snorted. "You wouldn't agree to that in a million years." He surveyed the items he'd spread out. "Your pack needs to be lighter. I don't want you arguing over that. It's because of the extent of your injuries, not because you *can't*. Got it?"

She wanted to argue, just out of spite or pride, but both had to be left behind. Elijah had started a fire at Duke's house, and even if he hadn't hurt people, he'd made it clear he could.

That couldn't continue.

She put the pack she'd found on the bed next to Brady's, then let him divvy up the supplies as he saw fit. She didn't let herself watch, because she would have argued.

"We'll get as close as we can to Flynn in the truck. It'll be a hike to get to the main camp."

"Yeah, but I don't think he'll expect us here. Even if we never show up at the ranches, he won't think we've come for him. He'll think we've only run farther away. He won't expect a direct attack. I don't think he could."

"No, I don't think he could," Brady agreed. "But, we have to be prepared if he does." Brady stood back and examined both packs, now full. He scratched a hand through his hair. "This could easily be a suicide mission. Even if the Sons are weaker than they were, the fact they're still inhabiting Flynn and not moving on to a new, smaller camp means they're not falling apart, or even factioning off from what we can tell."

"The camp wasn't at Flynn when you were a kid."

"No. Flynn is Ace's origin story. It's where he was abandoned. It's his mecca, and it's where he tried to make us all into Wyatt men." Brady rolled his shoulders as if to physically move past those old, awful memories. "He built camp there this year to make his final stand…or something. Didn't quite go as planned for him."

"And if Elijah is Ace's son, he might be the cohesive reason they're not splitting off."

Brady nodded grimly. "Exactly."

He was being stoic. Planning and trying to figure the situation out, but the weight of what he would be facing hung over him. "I know this is hard for you."

Brady shrugged that away. "Jamison did it. To save Gigi. I can do it."

"The ability to do something and the toll it takes to do something aren't the same."

His gaze met hers over the bed. "If you're trying to talk me out of something, you don't know me very well."

"Situation reversed, you'd do the same thing, only you'd tell me you were trying to protect me."

"Is that what you're trying to do?"

She shrugged much like he had. "Maybe." It felt

a little uncomfortable. After all, Brady was bigger, stronger and more versed in what the Sons could do than she was. It seemed kind of ludicrous, even with her law enforcement background, that she *could* protect him.

But the more she learned about his horrifying childhood, the more she wanted to at least shelter him from that.

"It won't affect my ability to get this done."

Cecilia frowned. Were all men this dense or only Wyatt men? "Maybe I was worried about something else."

"Like what?"

"Like your *feelings*, Brady."

His eyebrows drew together like he didn't understand how that could possibly be a concern.

Which irritated her enough to say something she'd planned to keep to herself. "When you care about someone, you care a little if they have to relive their childhood trauma."

He stared at her for a minute before skirting the bed. She wanted to run away. To forget they'd ever had a conversation about anything. There were far bigger problems than *feelings*.

But he came right up to her and touched her cheek. "I'd relive a hundred childhood traumas for that innocent baby. For my brothers. For the Knights. For a lot of people."

Outrage and hurt chased around inside of her

chest, leaving her unable to speak or move. He'd do it for *anyone*. Fine and dandy.

"It would be my duty, no question. But I'm doing this not just as a duty, Cecilia. Not just because you'd do it without me or because God knows you need someone making sure you take as much care of those injuries as possible."

His fingers traced her jaw, causing a shiver to snake through her even as she tried to stand tall and unmoved. He had just told her he'd do this for *anyone*, as if that wasn't some kind of warped slap in the face.

"I love my brothers with everything I am, but because of how we grew up there…we have to protect each other. Have to. I'm sure we've all felt a certain level of protectiveness for you girls, but it's not the same. Early on I had to accept I can't save or protect everyone."

"What is your *point*, Brady?" she muttered, wishing she had the wherewithal to pull away from his hand gently caressing her cheek.

"The point is there's no obligation here. Not really. I could convince myself I don't need to help you but that would be denial. Because in the end, for whatever reason, I want to be by your side for your fights, and I want you by my side for mine. Not blood, not obligation, not shared crappy history, but because you're the person I need. Because there's something here. I wouldn't say I would have chosen that, but there's no turning back now."

Cecilia didn't often find herself speechless, but that just about did it. Words were not her forte, more so, she didn't think they were particularly Brady's forte. But he'd laid it all out. Honesty complete with uncertainty of how or why, but a certainty it existed.

And he was still touching her face, watching her like there was anything she *could* say.

She cleared her throat. "When this is over…" She didn't know what she was trying to say. Or maybe she did and just didn't want to admit it to herself. The words stuck in her scratchy throat anyway.

Brady pressed a kiss to her forehead, briefly rested his cheek on the top of her head. "Let's get it over, first."

Which somehow wasn't the answer she wanted. Or the reassurance. "Just know, if you take it all back, I'll kick your butt to Antarctica *and* tell your family you're a turd."

A smile tugged at his lips despite the pressing, dangerous circumstances. "Deal."

Chapter Sixteen

Brady did best with a specific goal in mind. The goal was to get to Elijah before they were expected. If he focused on that goal, he didn't think about how close he was to stepping into his own personal hellscape, or that Cecilia was seriously compromised by her injuries.

It was still dark when they reached as close to the Sons camp as he dared go by truck. The sky to the east hinted at the faint glow of dawn, but the stars still shone brilliantly above the inky dark of the shadowy Badlands.

It was beautiful and stark and it had Brady's chest tightening in a vise. His father had believed this land had anointed him some kind of god, and so Brady had never had any deep, abiding love for it.

But he remained, didn't he? He could have moved. He could have left South Dakota altogether, but he still lived just a quick drive from the place where all his nightmares had been born.

He wasn't sure what that said about him, and knew he didn't have time to figure it out now.

"Jamison and Liza did their best to give me an idea of the different areas of camp. Liza wasn't familiar with Elijah—not as a member, or a high-ranking official."

"What about as Ace's potential son?" Cecilia asked.

Brady shook his head. "I didn't bring it up, but she would have told Jamison if she'd heard anything like that."

"And you think Jamison would tell you?"

"Maybe not before, but knowing Elijah is after Mak and we're after Elijah? Yeah. He would. He'd have to."

"So, we have an idea of how the camp is laid out. Any idea where we find Elijah in it?"

"Depends. What Liza described to me isn't all that different than the camps when I was a kid. Different location, but same basic tenants. There were a few more permanent residences than the Sons are used to, but those were blown up a few months ago by North Star."

Cody had been part of North Star, a secretive group working to take down the Sons of the Badlands, and had delivered the first devastating blow to the Sons by taking out some of their higher-ranking members and arresting Ace, but still the Sons continued to exist, and cause harm.

Brady considered what he knew about the gang both from growing up within its confines, his work as a police officer, and what Liza had told him during their phone call.

"My guess is they constricted. Got closer together. That'll help. But I don't know where Elijah fits in the hierarchy. Ace was still in charge when Liza was there."

"He has men he can send after us. Doesn't that put him high up?"

"I think so. The guy with the gun yesterday—I recognized him. Not by name, but I remember that face. He's not just Elijah's man, he's been a Sons member for a while. Elijah has to be some kind of leader to have veteran members doing his bidding."

"Unless it's a coup. Maybe he's trying to overthrow Ace? He's recruited men in the Sons like he recruited some kids from the rez?"

"Could be. One thing we know is that with Ace in jail, the foundations of the Sons have been shaky. Cody overheard them talking about power vacuums a few months ago."

"Maybe Elijah filled it."

"Maybe." Brady took a deep breath. "It's the hypothesis I'm going to work off of, and it just so happens I know where the powerful men of the Sons congregate."

She shifted in the seat. They were sitting in the dark so he couldn't see her face, but he didn't really want to. He didn't like to be reminded of his father's former standing in the Sons. He didn't imagine other people found it very comfortable either.

"You know, I don't know anything about my father. He could be the leader of some gang somewhere. He could be a murderer. He could be a million terrible things."

"The difference is I do know. I appreciate you trying to comfort me, but I know exactly what my father is and what he's done." Probably not everything, but certainly enough to be haunted by it.

"And I know exactly who you are and what you'll do." Her hand found his in the dark of the truck.

He squeezed it. They needed to get going, put some distance in before the sun rose. He kept her hand in his. "I need you to promise me that you'll be honest with me about the state of your injuries. If things hurt. If there's bleeding—or bleeding through bandages. You have to let me know when we need to stop and take care of those issues. I need you to promise."

She was quiet for a few humming seconds, and he waited for the lie or the argument.

"All right," she said gravely, with enough weight and time between his words and hers for him to believe her. "I promise."

He gave her hand a squeeze. "Then let's get going."

They both got out of the truck, loaded their packs on their backs, and set out into the rocky landscape before them.

Brady had his cell phone on silent, though the service out here would be patchy at best. He had a mental idea of the area that hadn't changed all that much since he'd been tasked with survival out here as a child. He had the pack on his back and he had an injured Cecilia hiking beside him in the dark.

Not exactly where he'd planned to be a few weeks ago, or months ago, or certainly after New Year's Eve.

He'd had some disdain for the way Gage and Felicity had gotten together. Brady could admit it now, in the privacy of his own thoughts. He'd understood Liza and Jamison, Nina and Cody—they'd had a history before going through their ordeals. But Felicity had been harboring a crush on Brady for he wasn't sure how long. Brady hadn't understood how dangerous situations gave way to honest, deep feelings.

No matter that he could see Gage and Felicity now and knew they were happy, he'd been skeptical.

But now he understood that danger and running stripped away the walls and the safety exits you built for yourself without fully realizing it. He'd been able to lecture Cecilia about kissing him on New Year's Eve because his life had been intact and he'd been able to use that as an excuse to wedge between them.

But danger—life or death danger. Worry—keeping a baby safe worry. These were the things that stripped you to nothing but who and what you were.

It was a lot harder to fight feelings here.

Brady took a deep breath of the canyon air. He didn't love the Badlands, and he didn't love the act of hiking—both brought back ugly memories of an unpleasant childhood. He preferred the rolling hills of the ranch or the sturdy, square grids of town.

Because in the dark, in the unusual shapes of the

Badlands built by rivers and wind, Brady knew the only thing they were really going to find was danger.

DAWN BROKE, PINK and pearly. A gentle easing of sun over dark. It felt like some kind of promise. Peace.

Cecilia knew Brady was keeping the hiking pace slow for her. Normally she would have chastised him for it, but everything hurt. Her feet, her body, her injuries—especially the stab wound. Her head pounded and even though he made her stop every so often and drink water, her mouth was miserably dry.

She was both hungry and nauseous and utterly, completely miserable. She walked on anyway, because Elijah or his men had set a fire at her childhood home with the people she loved most in the world inside.

She glanced at the man in front of her, bathed in the golden light of sunrise.

Love was a very strange, complicated word. She adjusted her pack, happy to focus on how heavy the light load felt rather than anything like *love*.

"Need a break?"

"No. No. Rather get this over with than break."

"I think we're close enough if we can get high enough, we can see the camp. I want to climb up here and try," Brady said, pointing to a large, steep rock outcropping. "You can stay put, be the lookout."

Cecilia shaded her eyes with her hand. The climb looked difficult even if she were in perfect health. Still, she didn't want to be down here caught off guard if someone came upon her, or vice versa. "Let's see what I can do."

"Favor that side," he instructed. Clearly he didn't want her to make the climb, but didn't want to leave her alone either. They started the climb, and Brady basically hovered over her trying to mitigate any effort to her side.

She wanted to be irritated, but she wouldn't have made it without his help. Even *with* his help, she felt more than a little battered when they reached the top. But she could almost put that aside when she looked out below.

This wasn't strictly national park land, but the Badlands still stretched out, all canyons and valleys with only the occasional patch of flat and grass. In the lowest valley, some distance off, there was clearly a camp of some kind

And while they were alone in *this* moment, it was clear people used the flat area of this rock outcropping. There was a lockbox dug into the ground, rocks pushed together to form a kind of bench. Signs of footprints.

"Lookouts," Cecilia muttered, toeing the locked box.

"Might have caught them during the dawn changing of the guard," Brady said, looking out over the valley below. "But they don't keep lookouts all the time. With their diminishing numbers they probably only do it when there's a threat."

"What would be considered a threat?"

"Cops or federal agents mostly. A few months before Jamison got Cody out, there was a big ATF investigation. Nerves were high. Always a lookout then."

She couldn't help but watch him when he offered little pieces of his childhood like that. It was purposeful. He'd never once spoken about his time in the Sons to her before, and so doing it now had to be because…

Well, because he'd decided to trust her. Or care about her. Or something.

He pointed to the camp below. "If Elijah has an actual position of importance, and I'm thinking he does, that's his compound right there to the north. He might not have the main tent, but he'd have a tent in that area."

"So we climb back down and hike around to the north side?"

"Not to the north, no. The main compound is more guarded than the rest. They'll have guards positioned all along the north perimeter to make sure no one tries anything. I think especially with all the factions and power issues, you're going to have a lot of presence there."

"We can't exactly cut through the camp."

"No. I'm too recognizable, and you may be too at this point. It's going out on a limb, but I don't think he'd be here right now. He's either at the rez, or close to the ranches. He's going to be somewhere he thinks we're going. So, our goal is to cut him off before he gets to the camp when he realizes we're not rushing home."

Brady pointed again, this time to the southern portion of the camp. "That's the main entrance. See how they've got it set up? You've got tire tracks coming in right there—and I don't see any other vehicle points of access. So, that's the road in."

"He's not going to be alone."

"No. And we can't just ambush him. All that does is land us in another fight, and it doesn't give us any grounds to arrest him."

"So, what are you proposing then?"

Brady finally took his gaze off the camp below. "Do you know how Jamison created a big enough distraction for me and Gage to escape?"

Cecilia wasn't sure she wanted to know. Every time he told her some awful story about his childhood she wanted to wrap him in a hug. Which wasn't exactly a comfortable reaction for her, even if she was coming around to the idea of...well, whatever she felt for Brady.

"He'd gotten Cody out almost two years before us. A few months before us, he'd gotten Tuck out. Obviously, the suspicion was that Jamison had orchestrated it, but no matter how Ace tried, he couldn't figure out how. He beat Jamison, he beat Gage, he beat Dev. He threatened, raged, demanded answers from the people around us, but he never could find actual evidence that Jamison was behind the escapes."

"Why didn't he beat you?" Cecilia asked.

Brady blinked. Then he turned away from the camp, made a move to climb down.

"Brady. I asked you a question."

"He believed me when I said I didn't know since he said I couldn't lie to save my life. It wasn't worth the energy to beat me." He held out his hand to help her down the first steep descent. She knew she should just take his hand, not react to that…horror.

But it was so *complex* in its horror, and the more she got a glimpse into what he'd endured the more in awe of him she was. No *wonder* he could be a little stuffy and standoffish. No *wonder* the rules meant so much to him.

Why on earth had he slept with *her*?

Which wasn't a question they had any time for.

"The point of the story is that Jamison created a distraction," Brady continued, waiting for her to take his hand. "He ambushed someone he knew had been working with the cops, called a Sons meeting and told Ace this was the man he'd been looking for."

Cecilia nearly stumbled as Brady helped her down. "Jamison threw someone under the bus?" She couldn't begin to imagine. He'd be right to. He and his brothers stuck in hell, she wouldn't blame Jamison a bit. Still, it surprised her.

"Not exactly. The guy *had* been working with the cops, but he'd gotten pissed off and killed one of them. So, while Jamison had set this meeting in motion, he'd also managed to send evidence to the local police department that this man was the culprit.

So, the distraction was twofold—finally finding the perpetrator, and the cops coming to the compound."

"That sounds complicated."

"It was. I don't know how many weeks he spent working it all out, getting the timing right. And he did it all on his own. Well, I think Liza helped him. We still almost got caught. All that and we still almost got caught." Brady shook his head as if he could shake away old, bad memories with it. "Anyway, point is we need that kind of distraction. Something to keep Elijah focused and busy on one hand, while we're working to arrest him on the other."

Cecilia looked around the vast landscape. The camp was now hidden behind the rocks to their backs. "How on earth are we going to do that?"

Brady paused. "Well, he wants both of us for different reasons. If he had one of us…"

Brady trailed off.

"You don't honestly think one of us could be a distraction?"

"It makes sense. One to distract, and one to observe the arrestable offense. And then move forward with the arresting."

"And let me guess—you think *you* should be the distraction?"

"Actually, no. I think it should be you."

Chapter Seventeen

Cecilia stared at him, mouth actually hanging open. She'd stopped her forward progress down the steep incline, but she still held on to his hand.

Brady couldn't say he *liked* his idea, but unfortunately it was the most sensible. He thought she would have seen that herself, but apparently not.

"Unfortunately it makes sense. You're hurt, which means it's going to be harder for you to be stealthy. It'd make more sense for you to pretend to be caught. I can move around easier, observe with more ease and care, *and* arrest with more force. Plus, your jurisdiction is limited to the rez. While we're outside Valiant County lines, I've got more of a legal standing than you. In a court of law."

She blinked, mouth still hanging open. When she finally spoke, it was only to echo his own words. "Court of law."

"It has to be legal, Cecilia."

She blinked again, multiple times, as if that would somehow change anything. "You're going to let me be a sacrificial human diversion. You said we'd never split up and you want to do just that."

"Let's not use the word *sacrificial*. All the elements have to come together right. Including making sure we've isolated Elijah before we allow you to be any kind of diversion. Then, it has to be absolutely certain I'll be able to follow, observe and arrest. Not split up, give the illusion of splitting up."

She finally started moving forward again, letting him take some of her weight on the way down. When they reached more even ground and a tuft of grass amidst the rocky terrain around them, he started leading her toward the best positioning for their purposes.

"We'll want to keep ourselves by the road, a ways away from camp. The biggest challenge right now is to figure out a way to block Elijah from getting to camp—and keeping him separate from camp if we do let him catch you."

"Let him catch me. You're going to *let* Elijah catch me."

"No, *I'm* not going to let him, Cecilia. You're going to either make the decision to be the diversion or not. If you don't want to do it, we'll devise a new plan." And part of him really wanted her to refuse, even though he knew she wouldn't. Even though this was the only way.

"We can't do this alone. It's just not possible with only the two of us. Not this close to literally *hundreds* of people who'd help him."

"What about three of us?"

At the sound of a third voice, Brady whirled, gun in hand. He hadn't heard a sound, even a potential for someone sneaking up on them. He was ready to shoot first and ask questions later, but the voice was too familiar.

Brady stared at his brother for a full twenty seconds, gun still pointed at him. "Tucker. How... Wh... What on earth are you doing here?"

Tucker's smile was easy, but it hid something that made Brady fully uneasy. "I'm a detective. I'm detectiving."

That didn't make any sense. Brady could only frown at Tucker. "This isn't your jurisdiction."

Tuck shrugged. "I needed to do some looking myself and get a grasp on what I'll need local law enforcement to do when we're ready to move. It's a pretty complicated case. Lots of departments and moving parts."

None of that made any sense, least of all Tucker having some case that tied to the Sons that none of them knew about.

"And you just *happened* to come across us here in the middle of nowhere?" Cecilia demanded, not even trying to hide her suspicion.

Brady didn't know how to be suspicious of his own brother, even when none of this felt right.

"It's not exactly the middle of nowhere," Tucker replied, unoffended. "It's the Sons lookout that gives the whole camp's layout." Tucker waved an arm as if to encompass the camp behind the large outcropping they'd just climbed down. "And now I can help you guys."

"How did you find us?" Brady returned.

"I'm not here for you, Brady. I mean, I can help. I want to. But it isn't why I was here. I was here for my job. I heard you guys and came closer. By the way, I listened to your plan and it kind of sucks without backup."

"I wouldn't call one more person backup," Cecilia replied, her demeanor still suspicious.

Brady could only feel conflicted. His gut was telling him that something was off, but this was Tucker. Tucker was… Probably the most well-adjusted out of all of them. He was good like Jamison, without Jamison's penchant for taking on too much responsibility. He worked hard like Brady without letting it make him too uptight. He had Gage's good humor without using it as a shield.

But none of this made sense, and Brady didn't like the fact Tucker was clearly lying to them. To *him*. When had Tucker ever lied?

"Elijah was camped out near the ranches. Had a small group with him. Only two other men that we could tell. The group or person who started the fire is gone, so he's traveling light. So if we can somehow take out his communication, three against three isn't such bad odds."

Brady opened his mouth to tell Tucker Cecilia was hurt and didn't count as a full person, but he found something so off-putting about all of this, he just closed it right back up. He couldn't put Cecilia at risk until this felt less...wrong.

"You can't be serious," Cecilia said. "You can't honestly think we buy any of this."

Some of the forced cheerfulness melted off Tucker's face. "But if you buy it, I can help." He turned his attention from Cecilia to Brady. "Surely you trust me to help."

Brady had never once questioned his brother's honesty or loyalty. Even as kids. Tucker was honest to a fault. On more than one occasion the Wyatt brothers had ganged up on Tuck for telling Grandma Pauline something she would have been better off not knowing.

Nothing about this felt right or honest, but it was *Tucker*. "Of course we do."

"Speak for yourself," Cecilia interjected. "You're acting fishy as hell. I don't trust that for a minute."

"Cecilia," Brady muttered.

"No, it's all right. She doesn't have to trust me." Tuck smiled. "But you trust me, Brady. Right?"

Never in his life had he hesitated to trust one of his brothers. It was alarming to hesitate now. But something wasn't right—and he didn't know how to figure out what.

CECILIA FELT A little bit like crying. Tucker Wyatt wasn't some Sons spy. She knew that in her gut, in her heart.

But her mind was telling her he was sure acting like one.

It didn't take anyone with some great understanding of Brady to see that the hesitation cost him. Hurt him. Hence the tears, because the idea of Brady being laid low by his brother's potential betrayal just ate her up inside.

But how could they trust Tucker with their lives when he very clearly wasn't telling the truth?

"I trust you, Tuck. How could I not?" Brady said, very gravely, very carefully as if every word was picked for greatest effect. "You've never given me a reason not to."

Cecilia kept her mouth shut, even though *shady appearance out of nowhere* was at the top of her list for not trusting him.

"My theory is they'll head back to camp this afternoon. They won't wait around at the ranches *too* long for you to show up, because if you're not going to rush back, you're probably not coming, right?"

"Were you there when Cody called me to tell me about the fire?" Brady asked, frown still in place.

"In the room? No. Dev and I were out searching for signs of Elijah's men."

"But you were home at the ranch when the fire started?"

"Well, yeah, we've all been taking turns keeping close. If we're all there it looks suspicious, so Jamison and Liza were back in Bonesteel with Gigi. Cody is having some guys work on his house so it looks like he and Nina and Brianna are staying with the Knights during renovations. And I come and go like I usually do, though I try to stick around a little extra time without being too conspicuous. That's what we planned from the beginning, isn't it?"

It all sounded good, and Tucker seemed at ease with the questioning and with his answers. Cecilia shouldn't have that gut feeling that something was all wrong.

But she did.

"We've got a few hours to set up some kind of… booby trap, for lack of a better word. Something that will stop Elijah from getting close to the Sons camp. Of course, our main problem is he could easily message for backup—and backup would come ASAP."

Brady helped her over a particularly unsteady part of the rock where she was struggling to get her footing. He didn't say anything, so she did the same. Tucker followed, as if happy to walk in utter silence with no feedback on his plan.

"We put out a few things that take his tires out. Then a little ways down the road we do some kind of…ambush? Trap? Something they can't get past. The only problem we're up against is their phones."

"Won't they immediately call for help if they blow out a tire? Before they even get out of the car?" Brady returned.

Tucker shrugged, continuing to follow them down closer to that makeshift road. "Depends on how in a hurry they are. Out here blowing a tire wouldn't be that uncommon. Probably used to it. No reason to get extra people when they'll have the ability to make a quick change themselves."

Cecilia studied Brady. He seemed to be considering Tucker's ludicrous argument. Brotherly love or not, Cecilia would not walk them into an ambush like that.

"That's ridiculous," Cecilia said forcefully. "Elijah wouldn't sit around waiting for the tire to be changed. Especially if he's trying to figure out why we didn't come chasing after him like he hoped. He'd call for another ride, or he'd walk it. He's not going to sit around and change a tire or wait for his men to."

Tucker didn't argue, but he didn't pipe up to agree with her assessment either. So, she kept talking. "It can't be something they need to be rescued from or can be helped out. It has to be their idea to get out of the car, without raising any red flags that might make them call ahead to the camp."

Tucker and Brady mulled this as they walked. When she hissed out a breath from landing too hard on her already aching leg, that sent a jolt of pain through her stab wounds, Brady held out a hand to help her again.

She noticed Tucker watched the exchange carefully, and it dawned on her that Brady hadn't mentioned her injuries to Tucker. It was pertinent information, especially as they made plans. But he'd avoided the topic.

Maybe he didn't fully trust Tucker either. Her heart twisted because she knew that had to be eating him up alive. To question one of his brothers. And if Cecilia was right in her gut feeling? If Tucker was up to something wrong?

The whole Wyatt clan would be…wrecked. There was no other word for it.

They walked farther in silence. Cecilia kept her eye on Tucker. Something was up with him. She didn't want to think it was nefarious, but what else could it be? If it was anything *good*, he'd tell them.

They were coming up on the path that worked as entrance into the camp now. "If I'm going to be the prisoner anyway, why not use me as a diversion here?" Cecilia pointed to the road a ways off.

"He might think something's fishy about stumbling upon you," Brady returned.

They all stopped and Brady passed her a water bottle, which earned another careful look from Tucker. Cecilia met his considering gaze and raised an eyebrow. Tucker only turned away.

Something was *really* not right here.

"We'd have to set it up. Make it look like I'm trying to get to camp, trying to not be seen, only we have to make sure he sees me. And doesn't see either of you."

Brady studied the area around them. "It's too open. Why would you be hiking through here when you could be in the rock formations?"

Cecilia considered Tucker. Her best idea was to milk her injuries, pretend like she was struggling to hike and needed the even ground. But Brady hadn't mentioned her injuries, and that had to be purposeful. So she flashed a fake smile at Tucker. "You mind giving us a few minutes?"

Tucker's eyebrows drew together. "Huh?"

"I want to talk to your brother in private. Without you listening. Can you go over there?" She pointed to some rocks in the distance.

"You can't be serious," Tucker replied, and his outrage didn't seem fake. That felt very real. The first real reaction he'd given since they'd "bumped" into him up on the lookout point.

It was good to see *something* could elicit a real response out of him. "I'm very serious. What I have to say to Brady is private. So…" She made a shooing motion.

Tucker turned his indignant gaze to Brady.

Brady sighed. "Just give us a few, Tuck. This isn't about you anyway."

Tucker's mouth firmed, but he walked toward the pile of rocks Cecilia had motioned to. And boy, did he not seem pleased about it.

Which, in fairness, could be his reaction whether he was trying to help or sabotage. The younger Wyatt brothers were never very good at being dismissed. Which was why she'd always gone out of her way to find ways to dismiss them.

She glanced up at the Wyatt brother still with her. He'd always handled it the best. With just enough disdain to irritate her right back. None of the carrying-on or male bluster, just a calm nonchalance that always had her losing her temper first.

That warm feeling was spreading through her chest again, but she had to shove it away and focus on the problem at hand. "I didn't want to say it in front of him, but if I overact my injuries, it might be a plausible enough reason for Elijah to believe I was taking the easy route in."

"Maybe, but only if it was dark. I don't think he'd believe you doing it midday. There'd be no reason."

Cecilia frowned. True enough, but if Elijah was coming back this afternoon, they didn't have time for that.

"Why'd you send him over there for that?" Brady asked.

"Why didn't you tell him I'm hurt?"

Brady scrubbed a hand over his face. "I...don't know."

"I know why, Brady. You didn't tell him because we can't actually trust him. Something isn't right about all this."

Brady's forehead lined and he stared at Tucker bent over the rock. "Maybe it's not right, but... I can't let myself not trust my own brother. Not Tuck. He wouldn't... He just wouldn't. Whatever is off is something he can't tell us, but that doesn't mean it's wrong or bad."

Cecilia frowned at him even as her heart pinched. She understood his loyalty, the need for it.

But she absolutely could not be caught in the cross fire of his misplaced loyalty.

Chapter Eighteen

Brady felt as though he was being pulled in two very correct directions. This was not black-and-white. There was no one clear, right answer.

He had to trust his brother. His younger *brother*. Tuck, who had always been good and dedicated to his law enforcement career, to taking down Ace and the Sons. Brady absolutely had to trust Tucker—it was the right thing to do.

Brady had also made a successful law enforcement career through listening to his gut, and the facts. Both the facts and his gut pointed to this being all wrong. Those things told him not to trust Tucker.

Then there was Cecilia. He'd made her sit down because she looked too pale. She was all but staring daggers at Tucker who was moving back over to join them.

"I have an idea," Tucker said grimly. "You probably won't like it."

"You're finally catching on," Cecilia muttered.

Tuck pretended not to notice. "The thing is, he expected you both to run back to the Knights after the fire. He expects you to be mad, right? Probably doesn't expect you to run to the Sons camp, but it wouldn't be out of the question for either of you to come after him directly. He wouldn't necessarily find it out of character if one of you were waiting here for a standoff."

"That'd be suicide," Brady replied.

"Would it though? I don't have any evidence Elijah has ever killed anyone. Do you?"

"We could say the same about Ace," Brady replied, resisting the need to rub his chest where that truth always lodged like a weight.

Tucker shook his head. "We know better. And sure, Elijah could use his goons as mercenaries to keep his hands clean. Ace did enough of that. But Elijah isn't Ace. He's not the leader of the Sons. He's trying, sure. Maybe he's even getting there. But he's lived his life outside the camp. No matter how involved he's gotten."

"He thinks we're dumb, Brady," Cecilia offered. "He thinks he's smarter than us. And I think he'd want to have a face-off. He'd want to talk. He wouldn't shoot first."

"But he could," Brady insisted. "We could let Cecilia stand out there in the middle of the road, ready for a showdown, and he could just flat-out kill her in two seconds. Not happening."

"*I* took Mak. *I* know where Mak is, and his goons didn't try to kill me. They tried to take me."

"Which is exactly why you wouldn't be stupid

enough to go after him. He might underestimate us, but I don't think he's going to be fooled by a stand-off with you."

"Not her," Tucker agreed. "Mak or no, I think the potential for Elijah killing her is certainly higher than not. He'd want to torture her a bit, but if she was antagonizing him, he'd be fine with just taking her out. You, on the other hand, are a Wyatt. Ace Wyatt's son. Ace might be in jail, but we both know he still has some power here. You're worth more alive than dead as a power move. Even if you were threatening him, if he could bring you into camp, make some kind of example out of you in front of the group members—"

"Yeah, no," Cecilia said firmly, pushing up from the rock with a wince. "We picked me to be the distraction for a reason."

"But it's not just you two anymore," Tucker said evenly. "You have me."

"If I'm not standing there facing Elijah, neither is he. End of story."

"You two seem really worried about each other."

"So what if we are, Tuck? Got a problem with wanting people to stay alive?" Cecilia returned, and clearly wasn't thinking of her injuries when she stepped toward Tucker threateningly, like she was ready to fight him.

Tucker didn't react except to move his gaze from Cecilia to Brady. "Would you do it?"

Cecilia whirled, her eyes all flashing fury. "Think

very carefully about how you answer that question, Wyatt."

Which gave him some pause. He didn't care for being ordered about in that high-handed tone, but the reason behind it was, well, care. She cared about him. Didn't want to see him taking unnecessary chances any more than he wanted to see her taking them.

The more they talked about variables, adjusted plans, the more he realized…he couldn't let any of them get caught by Elijah. It was too much risk.

"He'd expect some kind of ambush if we were the aggressors," Brady said, carefully avoiding Tucker's direct question. "No matter how stupid or emotional he thinks we are, he'll suspect there are more of us waiting."

Tucker's expression was inscrutable, and the awful *don't trust this guy* feeling burrowed deeper. Tucker was never inscrutable, except at work. He had said this was work. But it was also life.

All three of them turned toward the sound of an engine. It was far off, carrying over the wide-open landscape around them.

"We don't have enough time for a plan. Just hide."

Tucker swore. "Where?" he muttered, whirling around. "You two, there," he said, pointing to the small pile of rocks. "Three of us can't fit, but I can run over to those."

Tucker didn't wait to see if Brady would agree. He started to run and Brady couldn't argue with him.

They didn't have time. He grabbed Cecilia's hand and they ran for the pile of rocks.

"If we're here they shouldn't see us unless they look back, which they'd have no reason to. You get situated in the most comfortable position. I'll get in around you."

"Just get out of sight, moron," she returned, settling herself behind the rock. He sat beside her. He'd need to sink lower.

"You need to be in a comfortable position that isn't putting too much pressure on that stab wound."

She muttered irritably under her breath, readjusted her position lying behind the rock, then he pretzeled his body to fit around her so they were hidden by the rock. Someone would really have to be looking for them to see them.

God, he hoped.

The engine was getting closer, though it was hard to tell how close the way noise moved and echoed in the vast valley. He could only keep his body as still as possible, focus on keeping his breathing even, and not crushing Cecilia.

Seconds ticked by, stretching long and taut, but he had been trained to deal with these kinds of situations. He couldn't think of what-ifs. He couldn't let his brain zoom ahead. He had to breathe. Steady himself and believe the car would pass. Everything would be fine.

He could tell the engine was getting closer, but how close was impossible to discern. He wouldn't be able to believe it was past them until he didn't hear it at all. So he focused on the even whir of the engine carrying on the air. Once it was gone, it would be safe.

A car door slammed above the low buzz of the engine. Both he and Cecilia jerked, almost imperceptibly. Training could keep them tamping down normal reactions, but it couldn't eradicate reflexes completely.

Cecilia's hand found his arm and she squeezed. Their breathing had increased its pace, but he could feel them both working together to slow it. In then out. Slow. Easy.

He couldn't hear over the pounding in his ears, or maybe there was nothing happening. Maybe the car door was miles away. Maybe they were overreacting.

"I saw something."

The voice was clear, close, and most definitely Elijah.

Brady listened as footsteps thudded. It sounded like the men Elijah was speaking to split up and went in different directions, but he couldn't be sure. He was tempted to risk a look, but Cecilia was still squeezing his arm as if to say *don't*.

Silence was intermittently interrupted by footsteps, the faint murmur of voices, or a scuttling sound that Brady eventually figured was rocks being kicked.

Then suddenly the sounds of a scuffle, maybe

even a punch and a grunt. Then a voice Brady didn't recognize.

"Found a Wyatt."

More footsteps—farther away from Brady. The sounds seemed to fade away, but he could just make out Elijah's words. "Well. This is an interesting development."

Cecilia's nails dug into his arm, as if she could keep him here. And it should. Brady should stay put. So, he held on to the fact that Tucker could take care of himself. He was smart. A detective. And a Wyatt, so like he'd said—more valuable alive than dead.

Elijah seemed surprised to have found him. Which meant whatever odd reason Tucker had for being here, chalking it up to coincidence, didn't have to do with the Sons.

Or does it just not have to do with Elijah?

"Not the Wyatt I expected, I have to say," Elijah's voice echoed through the midday heat. "Of course, where there's one, there's usually more."

"Yeah. Probably," Tucker replied, sounding almost cheerful. "Home sweet home, you know?"

Cecilia's intake of breath was sharp and audible. Brady shook his head just a bit, even though he doubted she'd see or feel it.

Tucker wasn't ratting them out. He was bluffing to Elijah so Elijah didn't go looking for them.

"Hurt him till he talks," Elijah ordered crisply. The order was immediately followed by a thud and a whoosh of breath.

Brady had to close his eyes, even though he couldn't see from behind the rock anyway. Tucker could take it. He could handle it.

Brady needed to stay put. Protect Cecilia. Tucker could take care of himself. This wasn't all that far off from what they'd been planning. Let him be taken, carefully follow. Arrest.

Tucker could handle it. Brady repeated that fact to himself as he heard the thud of blows, the grunts of pain. This was still better than sending an injured Cecilia to do the job.

He opened his eyes as the sound of fighting increased.

Brady couldn't stand it. He simply couldn't listen as Tucker got beaten by three men. Even if they kept him alive, they could do anything to Tucker, and Brady couldn't live with himself if he just…stayed put. He tried to move, but Cecilia's fingernails dug into his arm.

"Let him get captured, Brady," she hissed as quietly as possible. "It's half our plan anyway. We'll save him after. We'll—"

Brady shook his head, taking her hand off his arm. He quietly got to his feet and quickly shook off his pack. Gently and as silently as possible, he knelt and set it next to her. He looked her in the eye. "I can't. I'm sorry. I just can't do it." He pressed a quick kiss to her mouth. "If it were you like we planned, I wouldn't have been able to do it either. I'm sorry."

Then he left her. She had weapons and a cell

phone and the chance to escape. Tucker didn't, and Brady couldn't let him go down alone.

CECILIA WAS SHOCKED into stillness for probably more than a minute. All their talk and debating about plans, and it had just gone up in smoke. Brady walked away, all grim determination.

I wouldn't have been able to do it either.

That echoed inside of her. He'd planned to let her get caught, but he would have never been able to go through with that plan. She wanted to be angry, furious. She wanted to march after him and drag him back behind this rock and their little bubble of pretend safety.

But she understood too well what he'd meant. She was half-convinced Tucker was on the wrong side of things, even now, and it was still hard to listen to someone she'd grown up with and cared about get beaten up.

If it was one of her sisters? She wouldn't have lasted even as long as Brady. Still, this was…suicide. Surely. Maybe Brady and Tucker could *fight* three men off, but Elijah's men had to have weapons. Maybe Brady and Tucker were somewhat protected by their Wyatt name, but if they fought back hard enough, would Elijah really care to keep them around to use them as examples to the other Sons.

And what could she do? There was no cell service out here. She could shoot, but that made her a target too, and if she was a target, how would they get out of this mess? Someone needed to be safe to find the option to *get* help.

She heard the sounds of fighting and closed her eyes, taking a steadying breath. She had to think clearly, without emotion clouding her judgment. Emotion would get all three of them killed. And probably only after Elijah tortured them.

Torture. Would Brady give under torture? Tell Elijah exactly where Mak was? She didn't think so. She thought he'd die first.

But Tucker? Once she would have put her utter faith into him, but not today. Not with his weirdness.

She couldn't let them get captured, or at least not for very long. But in order to figure out what she was going to do, she had to look. She had to know what was going on to make an informed decision.

Maybe it'd be easy to get a shot off, to pick all three men off and end this here and now. It was possible, but she wouldn't know it unless she risked being seen.

She unholstered her weapon, and took another slow breath, calming her heart rate, trying to keep her limbs from shaking. Slowly, she peeked over the rock.

Tucker and Brady were holding their own in the fight. Brady was a little worse for the wear, probably since he'd already been beaten up the day before. But he and Tucker worked together like a team to take on the other two men, who fought like individuals. Elijah's men landed blows on Brady and Tucker, but they didn't make any headway on actually taking Brady or Tucker down.

Both of Elijah's men had guns strapped to their legs, but they didn't use them. Why not even use them as a threat? Brady was living proof you could shoot a man and have him survive. Why wouldn't they use the strongest weapons they had at their disposal?

"Why does none of this make sense?" Cecilia muttered to herself. She lifted her gun, trying to test if she could make two successive shots and take down both men before they returned fire.

There was too much struggle, though. She'd be just as likely to hit Brady or Tucker with the way they were all moving and stumbling and swinging at each other. And she wasn't guaranteed to make a glancing blow either. What if she missed altogether?

Wait. Two against two. Why were there only two men? Where was Elijah?

She looked toward the car Elijah and his men had left in the middle of the path to camp. It was still running, but she didn't see anyone. Had Elijah walked on to camp, leaving his lackeys to handle the Wyatt brothers? No. He wouldn't have done that.

There was a crack of sound behind her, like a gun being cocked, then the cold press of metal against the back of her head. She froze.

"Well hello, Cecilia," Elijah's voice said softly in her ear. "Didn't see this coming, did you?"

He peeled the gun out of her hand, and she had to

let him. Because she had no doubt Elijah would pull that trigger if she provoked him.

"Now. On your feet. We have so much to talk about."

Chapter Nineteen

Brady took another ham-fisted punch to the kidney and nearly lost his balance, but Tucker was there, backing him up, blocking the next blow and landing one of his own.

All of them were breathing heavily, not doing much more than landing punches that hurt but didn't take anyone out or down. Brady's gun had been knocked out of his hand before he'd been able to get a clear shot, and Tucker had lost his long before Brady had come to help.

It felt…pointless, Brady realized, ducking another punch with enough ease dread skittered up his spine. "Something isn't right," he muttered to his brother.

Tucker dodged a blow, landed a decent fist to one of the men attacking them.

One of the *two* guys. There were only two.

"Where'd Elijah go?"

Tucker swore, and not half a second later landed an elbow to one guy's temple that had him crumpling. In a fluid, easy move and with absolutely no help from Brady, he managed to get the other in a choke hold.

Had Tucker been…holding back?

No time to think about that. He let Tucker deal with handcuffing the two debilitated aggressors and searched the area around them for Elijah. Nothing.

He looked over to the rocks where Cecilia should be out of sight. Instead, past the rocks, he saw two figures. They were far away so he couldn't make them out well enough to be certain it was Elijah and Cecilia, but who else would it be?

"Go ahead," Tucker said. "Follow. I'll be right behind you. We can't have these guys coming behind us, and we have to see where he takes her. Go."

"No, Tuck. You don't follow me. You go get help. We can't do this alone. We need backup. You have to go get backup." His brother hadn't been acting normal. His actions didn't make sense, but Brady had to be able to trust Tucker. "Promise me."

Tucker was kneeling, tying the men's feet together with rope Brady had no idea how he'd gotten. "You could both get killed in the time it'll take me to get help. You don't even have a gun," he returned, not meeting Brady's gaze.

"We'll take our chances." Brady was already walking away from Tucker, toward Cecilia. He didn't have time to search for the one that had been knocked out of his hand or he'd lose sight of Cecilia. "We don't have *any* if we both go in there. But we do if you get help. We can arrest him. He's taken Cecilia against her will. We have arrestable grounds. All we need is enough law enforcement to make it happen."

He was running by the time he was done talking. Cecilia and Elijah had disappeared behind a large rock formation. Brady headed for the rock first, thinking to grab the pack quickly on his way.

But there was a fire. Small and it wouldn't spread thanks to the rocky landscape, but both his and Cecilia's packs were in the middle of the blaze. There was no chance of saving anything or finding a weapon.

Brady didn't stop to think about the implications, and while he considered the fact that Elijah could just shoot him dead in the middle of the Badlands, it didn't really matter.

If he'd wanted him dead, Brady could have been dead multiple times. He had to bank on the fact that either Ace's shadow, or potential family loyalty, or *something* was keeping Elijah from taking him out.

Maybe that wouldn't extend past an attack, or an attempt to get Cecilia back, but it was a risk Brady was willing to take.

And if Tucker doesn't get help?

Brady slowed his pace. It was an irrational fear. His brother had taken down those two men, fought beside him. Tucker would go get help.

He could have ended that fight a lot quicker.

Whatever it meant, whatever weird thing was going on with Tuck, it didn't mean he was helping

Elijah or the Sons. Brady had to stop letting stupid doubts plague him.

Even with Cecilia's life at stake?

It was too difficult a choice. Trust his brother over all else? Risk Cecilia over it? There was too much at stake to make an error.

He could only focus on himself. On what he could do.

He'd laid out a plan where Cecilia was captured, and even though he wouldn't have been able to *let* it happen, it was currently happening. And he was following, just like he'd planned. With or without backup, he could arrest Elijah. He had grounds.

All he had to do was catch up, somehow get Elijah away from Cecilia without her getting hurt and arrest him…with no weapon, no handcuffs and no help whatsoever.

He'd eased into a brisk walk instead of an all-out run. With the dust and rocky debris, there was a decent enough trail to follow as long as the wind didn't pick up and Elijah didn't realize Cecilia was digging her heels in and making enough of a track for him to follow.

Occasionally, he paused to listen to try and figure out how close he was, but he never got close enough to hear actual footsteps or the struggle Cecilia must be putting up.

She wouldn't go easily. Even if Elijah had a weapon. She wouldn't just docilely be marched along. Which meant, surely, Elijah had no plans to kill her either.

Brady wasn't sure how long he'd walked, following a trail, and not getting close enough to hear a scuffle before the landscape started to feel…more familiar. Too familiar. Bad familiar.

Brady stopped short. He knew this area too well. Old memories tried to surface, but he couldn't give them space. Couldn't give them power.

Couldn't allow himself to picture Ace on that rock above, throwing knives. Leaving him out here, seven years old and all alone.

Brady looked at the towering rock around him, preparing his body for that searing pain out of nowhere, as if he expected Ace to jump out and do what he'd always done. Brady wouldn't put it past Ace to share with Elijah how he'd tortured his children.

Ace had tortured them each in different ways, and they'd each kept that a secret from each other, thinking it was an individual personal shame. After Gage's ordeal, he'd told Brady about the ways Ace had tortured him.

Gage's admission had prompted them all to share their secrets. Which Ace wouldn't know. He'd think those secrets were ammunition, and wouldn't it make sense for Elijah to have been given all the ammunition to hurt Brady and his brothers?

Maybe Ace was in jail, but that didn't mean Elijah couldn't put men up there, armed with knives and Brady's nightmares.

The trail led right through the narrow chasm of rocks where Ace had often left Brady, only to torture him later. Where Brady had been forced away from his brothers to survive. On his own. As a child.

When he had nightmares, they all took place here, no matter how incomprehensible his dreams might be. Following that trail would be walking into his own personal hell.

I'll never go back there. Not for any reason. That's a promise I'm making to myself and I won't ever break it. No matter what.

He could hear his own words, spoken to his brothers, to his grandmother, to anyone who'd listen during that first year they'd all been out and with Grandma and *living* a real life.

Brady could stop here. He could go back. He could wait for help. He didn't have to brave his own personal hell.

Except Cecilia was at the end of this trail, and no matter what that twelve-year-old had told himself, there were reasons you broke promises to yourself. Reasons you did the things that scared you the most.

And that reason boiled down to one thing, always. A thing Ace didn't understand, and Elijah probably didn't either.

Love.

EVERYTHING IN CECILIA'S body hurt. Which wasn't new, it was just worse when there was a gun to her head and she knew Brady would come after her and they could both end up dead.

She tried not to let herself think like that. Fatalism *could* be fatal in her current situation. She needed to believe in Brady, and Tucker and even herself, that they could find a way to survive this.

No matter what hurt, no matter how impossible it seemed, she had to believe or she'd never find a way to survive this.

"Ah, here we are," Elijah said as if he were a waiter showing someone to their reserved table. Instead it was a tower of rock interrupted by a small crevice.

Without warning, he shoved her into that opening hard enough she stumbled and fell to her hands and knees. Which would have been his mistake if her body was cooperating. She would have immediately jumped up and disarmed him.

But her arms gave out on her so she fell onto her side, unfortunately her bad one, which hurt so badly she had to fight back tears and an encroaching blackness that wanted to take her away.

But she fought both away, breathing through the pain and the frustration. At first she'd thought he'd pushed her into a cave, but above her was bright blue sky. The air was hotter here, like the rocks were trapping it between them or radiating heat. She desperately wished she had her pack and could drink some water.

Though if she were wishing things, she supposed

she should be wishing she wasn't here at all. Or that she'd shot Elijah before he'd snuck up on her.

"On your feet now."

Cecilia grimaced, but did as she was told. If it came down to it, she'd fight and run, but for now it seemed in her best interest to listen to him.

"You're bleeding," Elijah offered, with a slight frown. He almost sounded concerned, but that tone was belied by the fact he was aiming a gun point-blank at her forehead as he moved closer to her, studying the red stain that had seeped through her gray T-shirt.

He stepped closer, reaching out. Cecilia braced herself for pain, for *something*. But all Elijah did was carefully lift her shirt and look at the stab wound.

Cecilia tried to control her breathing, tried to keep a handle on her revulsion. She failed. Miserably. No matter that it was preferable to say, being shot, it was creepy. It made her skin crawl as he kept her shirt lifted and studied the wound.

"You really should have gotten some medical attention for that. No stitches?" He tsked, lifting his gaze to meet hers. "What *were* you thinking."

She didn't answer him. Why would she? Still, she kept his gaze rather than stare at the gun that was so close to her forehead she could hardly think about anything else.

"You know, Layla quite liked being hurt," he said mildly. "Maybe you two have that in common."

"And maybe I puke all over your shoes."

Elijah lifted a shoulder as if it were of no concern of his. "I don't mind a little force, a little hurt, but you would invariably do something stupid, and as much as you fancy yourself the center of this, I'm not here for you."

She tried not to show her confusion, but Elijah's smile told her she'd failed.

"Don't worry. Brady will appear soon enough, ready to swoop in and save the day." He tapped his wrist. "I'm surprised it's taken two Wyatts this long, though. I wonder why it *did* take so long. Seems odd. Two strong, perfectly able-bodied men working together. Almost as if they, or one of them, wasn't trying to take the men out."

Cecilia's blood went cold. She refused to take anything Elijah said at face value, but could that mean Tucker was working for Elijah?

Please God, no.

She didn't speak until she knew she could do it and sound steady. Strong. "Brady will come with backup, and then where will you be?"

"He won't come with backup." Elijah let out a snort. "He'll run after you immediately. Especially since you're hurt. Wyatts and their noble pride are endlessly predictable."

"And yet alive. All six of them. And not incarcerated, unlike a certain Wyatt." Still, Elijah's words created some doubt. Surely Brady wouldn't come after her without backup... Except, wasn't that what he'd done with Tucker? Taken off to help without thinking about how he'd get himself out of it.

No. He'd expected *her* to get them out of it. So, she had to. Somehow.

"You know, Cecilia, you're making a grave mistake if you think I'm like Ace or your average thug. Killing leads to jail time. You don't always need to *kill* someone to get what you want."

She eyed the gun. If he wasn't going to kill her...

His smile was slow and self-satisfied. "Now, don't get too excited. Killing is often an excellent plan when it certainly can't be traced back to you. Which is why we'll wait for Brady's grand entrance."

"We know you're Ace's son." It was a gamble. Maybe it would make him more inclined to kill her. But maybe it would set him off-balance enough to give her a chance to best him.

Instead, Elijah laughed. If they were in a different situation, she would have believed it an honest, cheerful, good-humored laugh. "You know I'm Ace's son. You *know* that, huh?"

"Yes, I do."

He leaned in close, so their noses almost touched and the steel of the gun touched her forehead.

"You know *nothing*, Cecilia. And you're smart enough to know that, deep down. You're in over your head. Completely lost and completely expendable. You think I care about a *baby* when I'm building an *empire*?"

Cecilia didn't know how to parse that. He wasn't

after Mak? Then what was the point of the fire? Of threatening her at the rez? Why on Earth were they *here* if not for Mak?

Whatever the reason, he wasn't lying when he said she was expendable. Which meant she had to tread very, very carefully.

Brady would have gone to get backup. He wouldn't have followed her half-cocked. Tucker wouldn't let him. He'd been impulsive when Tucker was getting beaten up so he'd waded in, but he would think before coming to her rescue. Or Tucker would.

If Tucker wasn't on the wrong side of things.

She had to close her eyes against the wave of debilitating fear, because God knew none of what she told herself was true.

Chapter Twenty

The heat was excruciating. Dehydration was likely, if not a foregone conclusion. Brady was surrounded by his own personal nightmare and he had lost Cecilia and Elijah's trail.

Brady stood in the middle of the vast Badlands and wondered where the hell he'd gone so wrong in his life. He'd tried to be good and do the right thing. He'd been *shot* helping Gage save Felicity. He was a good man.

Why did he have to be a failure?

Failure or no, he couldn't give up. Not while there was a chance Cecilia was still alive. He couldn't have fully lost the trail. He'd made a wrong turn was all.

He backtracked, wiping the sweat off his face with his shoulder. He went back to the last place he saw the trail. It didn't end abruptly so much as got fainter and fainter. Perhaps a breeze had blown through and made the track lighter.

He stopped where he absolutely couldn't be certain it went on, then stood still and studied the land around him. All rock. All gradients of brown, red and tan broken up by the occasional tuft of grass. But there was a familiarity here, like there'd been in that corridor of rock earlier.

He was somewhere near…something he recognized. He couldn't place it yet, but he would.

Then he heard a thud. The lowest, quietest murmur of voices. It would be hard to tell where it was coming from the way sound moved in the Badlands, but he used the direction of the trail and his own instincts to propel him forward.

Then, as landmarks became clearer, he realized he didn't need to use either. He knew this place again. He knew where Elijah would have taken her.

There was no way Elijah wasn't Ace's son if he knew all Ace's spots. All Ace's ways of torture. They had to be linked *somehow*.

Brady took a moment to pause, to send up a silent prayer that Tuck would get backup and manage to find them in time, then moved quietly toward the entrance of the circle of rock.

But Elijah poked his head out of the small entrance between the rocks. "Welcome," he greeted sunnily. "Come on inside. Have a chat." Elijah cocked his head. "Unless you want her brain matter splattered across the rocks. Can't say *I* do, but I'll oblige if necessary."

Brady stepped into the wall of rocks. It was where he and Gage had hidden during their escape. It was where Andy Jay, a random member of the Sons, had taken pity on them and lied to their father, allowing them to continue on to Grandma Pauline's.

Brady had no doubt it was where Andy Jay had died at his father's hand, as punishment for letting them go. Andy's son hadn't forgiven the Wyatt brothers for their role in his father's death. He'd tried to take down Cody not that long ago and failed.

Brady couldn't think about that. His sole purpose was not letting Cecilia die here too.

He didn't do more than give a quick glance to make sure she was all right before he turned his attention to Elijah. Brady positioned his body between the gun Elijah was pointing and Cecilia.

Elijah rolled his eyes. "Do you really have to be so noble? It's boring and predictable. I can shoot her regardless of what you do, so take a seat next to her like a good little soldier and we'll keep her brain intact."

Brady considered rushing him. They were in a small enclosed space, and Cecilia would back him up, even injured.

But if he could keep Elijah talking, he might get more information to use against Ace. To keep Elijah in jail longer, and to bide time until Tuck got back with reinforcements.

If Tuck comes back with reinforcements.

Brady took a careful seat next to Cecilia on the rock. She looked pale. He noted the splotch of blood on her shirt. She was bleeding through her bandages, surely dehydrated, and nothing about the situation they were in was good for that.

"If you don't think I've figured out you're Ace's son, you're not as smart as you think you are."

Elijah laughed, enough to make Brady…uncomfortable. He was certain it was true, but Elijah's laugh was…off.

"I'm not Ace's son," Elijah replied, keeping the gun trained on Cecilia's head.

"Is that what he makes you say? I wonder why it's gotta be such a secret."

Elijah shook his head. "See, I was chosen, Brady. I wasn't just born. Ace picked me. He saw something in me. He didn't knock up some dim-witted gang groupie and have some warped sense of loyalty because of *blood*. I was chosen because I'm better. Smarter. I can see things people like you never will."

"You mean you were his brand of crazy and you listened to what he said?"

Elijah's humor was quickly sliding away. His eyes went icy, his grip on the gun tightened, and his smile turned into a sneer.

"You're his weakness. The lot of you. You aren't the reason he's in jail. His delusion that one of his blood-born children would take over the Sons is what got him there. Blood. As if that matters. I will take over the Sons." Elijah tapped his chest. "I'll leave Ace behind if I need to. I'm the next in line because he saw something in me, and I'm the best prospect to take over."

"I'm not part of the Sons. What do I care if you're

better? It'll always be my job to take down the illegal activity in my jurisdiction."

"You're a part of Ace, which means that you're currency, Brady. Not important, but usable. Taking you out was an option, but it doesn't send the message I want. I don't want blood and destruction like Ace. No, I want the Sons to be a real machine. Murder leads to anger and revenge and all that nonsense with Andy Jay and his son coming after you. I don't want that. I want consensus. I want loyalty."

"What about Mak?" Brady asked, to draw out the conversation but also because he didn't understand what any of this had to do with Cecilia.

"I don't care about that kid. I don't care about *blood*. Being chosen is what matters." Elijah took a deep breath as if to calm himself. "But I don't appreciate being *stolen* from. Sometimes you have to make a statement. Besides, I've studied you. I know your weakness." The gun pointed at Cecilia. "Damsels in distress. Long as I have a gun to her head, you'll do what I say."

"But I won't," Cecilia returned.

"You will. Because he wants you to."

"This is a really terrible plan, even for you," Brady muttered. Cecilia gave him a look as if to say *back off*, but Brady knew this kind of delusional behavior. He'd grown up under its highs and lows.

Anger would create an unstable environment, and Elijah might lash out, but he'd also lose sight of his plan.

"We've got two against one here. I've got more

help on the way. You'll never win." Brady shifted, trying to get his feet beneath him in a better position so he could lunge at Elijah.

He could take him out before he could shoot Cecilia. If he got a shot off, he'd hit Brady. Surely it could give her enough time to finish the job. He glanced at Cecilia. She was still too pale, and looked a little shaky, but she gave him a nod as if she knew what he was thinking.

Elijah lifted the gun and pointed it at Brady. His hand shook, color was rising in his face. "You're very lucky killing you isn't part of my plan."

Brady was pushing too far. He should stop, but his own anger was swelling up inside of him. That this continued to be his life. Tormented by power-hungry men, invested in being smarter and more important than everyone else.

Even when Ace was in maximum-security prison, Brady was fighting back the things Ace wrought, and he was tired of it.

"Face it, Elijah. You're a crappy leader. Your son will grow up knowing you were right about one thing, though. Blood doesn't matter."

"Crappy leader? I will rule the Sons, and they will reach more glory than they've ever known. He *chose* me."

Brady shrugged, ready to strike. "Ace chose wrong."

Brady leapt, but in that same second, Elijah's gun went off.

THE SOUND OF the gun echoed in the chasm they were in, followed by a howl of pain. Both men were on the ground, grappling, but Cecilia wasn't sure which was moaning in pain, or if they both were.

She couldn't see the gun either. Just a tangle of limbs rolling across the rocky ground.

The rocks. Cecilia lunged for the biggest one she could hold. She'd just need one clear second and she could bash Elijah over the head.

But there was no opportunity. There were only grunts and groans of pain. She saw blood, but couldn't tell who it came from. Her stomach turned, but she had to focus on getting Elijah's gun.

Screw the rock and her own injuries. She had to get in there and do what she could. When Elijah was on top, she grabbed his hair and pulled. He reached back with the hand holding the gun, and she grabbed it by the barrel, trying to point it anywhere but at her and Brady.

Out of the corner of her eye she saw Brady scoot out from under Elijah. Elijah had one hand still wrapped around Brady's leg, but Brady kicked it until he shook off Elijah's grasp.

The blood was Brady's. It was already soaking through his pants leg, but Cecilia couldn't focus on that when she was grappling over the one gun in this godforsaken place.

She tried to rip the gun out of Elijah's grasp, but he held firm. With his other hand free, he swung up and landed a blow right on her stab wound.

The pain knocked her to her knees, but she kept her grip locked on the gun. She couldn't give in. She wouldn't give in.

Elijah was trying to scramble to his feet, pulling the gun with him, but she held fast. She used her whole body weight to keep the barrel pointed down rather than at her.

"You're going to die," Elijah said as he huffed and puffed and wrestled over the gun. "I'm going to make sure of it."

Pain screamed through her, but this was life or death. She had to try to shut out the pain and focus on getting the gun away from the man who would most definitely kill her, and then probably Brady too. If he hadn't already.

She couldn't let it happen. There had to be a way to survive.

She saw out of the corner of her eye Brady try to get to his feet, only to fall to his knees. She couldn't let the fear he'd been irreparably hurt weaken her limbs or her resolve. She needed to get the gun so she could get help for Brady.

It's a lot of blood.

She adjusted her footing, still pulling down on the barrel of the gun, as Elijah readjusted his grip. She kicked out, managing to land a decent blow. Elijah didn't go down quite the way she'd hoped, but she got a better handle on the gun. With one more yank she could—

Brady grabbed her, pulling her off Elijah, which

wrenched the gun from her grasp. She wanted to protest, but it was lost as he pushed her out of the opening at the same time something exploded.

Reflexively, she ducked and covered her ears. Rock rained down on them and Brady tried to cover her body with his. She shoved ineffectively at him. *He'd* been shot. She should be covering him.

From…an explosion? She finally managed to dislodge Brady from on top of her and looked at where she'd been not a minute ago.

The rocks had exploded. There was little more than rubble on two sides.

How… How?

She looked around the rest of the area, stopping short at the figure standing a few yards opposite the explosion site.

Tucker.

She blinked at him. Was she hallucinating?

"What on earth just happened?" Her ears rang, so her words sounded muted and far away. She looked at Brady. He was sitting on the ground, leaning against a wall of rock, injured leg out in front of him.

There was so much blood. So much…

Tucker handed her a strip of fabric. He must have torn it off his own shirt. She took it and wrapped it around Brady's leg.

"Let me guess, you need a hospital," Tucker said grimly, looking down at Brady's seated form and bloody leg with a certain amount of detachment.

The rubble behind them seemed to be of no consequence to him.

The words were still heard through a muffled filter, but Cecilia *could* make them out.

"Wouldn't hurt," Brady returned, his voice strained as Cecilia pressed the cloth Tucker had handed her to his wound.

"Ambulance is getting as close as it can. Paramedics will take the rest by foot and will be here any minute." Tucker's gaze moved from Brady to Cecilia. "You'll both be transported. Depending on Elijah's status, he might need to go first. And I'm not putting the three of you in the same ambulance."

"Shouldn't you…" Cecilia trailed off because she realized there were two people moving the rubble. Where had they come from?

Cecilia looked at Brady. His complexion was gray, but his eyes were open and alert.

"Elijah didn't think you'd get backup."

His mouth tugged upward ever so slightly. "I'm stupid, but not that stupid. Sent Tuck."

Cecilia looked back up at Tucker. She really thought he'd been against them, but here he was with backup.

Apparently the kind of backup who could explode rocks. She frowned. "How did you…"

Tucker shook his head. "Keep the pressure on that. You seem in better shape. I'm going to go help the paramedics find us."

He walked off and Cecilia looked at Brady. He

was so gray and so still. "I hope you're not entertaining any grand plans of dying, because that's not going to work for me."

His mouth tugged up at one corner. "Nah. Surviving close range gunshot wounds is my specialty. You know what they say. Getting shot twice in a year is lucky."

"No one says that, Brady."

"Well, unlucky would be dead, and I am not that."

The word *dead* gave her a full body shudder, so she rested her forehead against his, still keeping the pressure on his wound. She let out a shuddered breath, and said what she never thought she'd say to a man. A near-death experience changed a girl, though. "I love you."

He let out his own shaky breath, and she just couldn't stand it. This. His hurt. Her hurt. God knew what had happened to Elijah, but here they were. Alive. Bleeding, but alive.

"So. You know, you better feel the same way or I'm going to kick your butt."

He chuckled, winced, made a half-hearted attempt to raise an arm that just fell by his side.

"And you can't die."

"Not going to die," he said, though he seemed incredibly weak. "Gage is never going to let me live this down after the hard time I gave him about Felicity." This time he seemed to focus all his energy and lifted his hand to briefly touch her cheek. "If

I'm a little out of it here for a few minutes, it's just the shock. I'm not going to die. Got it?"

She swallowed down the lump in her throat and nodded.

"But you can be sure that I love you too. Because God knows I'd be a lot more pissed about getting shot again if it wasn't with you."

"That doesn't make any sense," she muttered, losing her battle with tears as one slipped over.

Brady opened his mouth to say something else, but one of the men by the rubble spoke first.

"He's alive."

Chapter Twenty-One

Brady had been shot before, and not that long ago. There was less fear this time. More irritable acceptance.

Cecilia was sitting next to him. A paramedic had done a quick patch job, but they were currently working on getting Elijah out of the rubble and onto a stretcher.

Brady had heard them mutter that if there was any hope of saving Elijah, he'd have to be transported ASAP. Brady's and Cecilia's injuries were serious, but they'd have to wait for a second transport.

"Why are they prioritizing saving him? He would have killed us," Cecilia muttered in Tucker's direction.

"Elijah might have some information that would... help my investigation."

Brady frowned at his brother. It was news to him he had any current investigation that connected to Elijah.

But there was something about this whole thing that made him keep his questions to himself.

The paramedics strapped Elijah to the stretcher, which would stabilize his body and keep him from being able to fight any of the paramedics, nurses or doctors who would deal with him on the way to the hospital.

His head was turned toward them as the paramedics walked by.

"There's so much worse coming for you Wyatts. So much worse," Elijah rasped. His face was bloody and torn up, but the hate in his eyes was clear and fierce.

"I think we'll handle it," Cecilia returned.

"Just like we've handled the rest," Brady added. If Ace kept coming, in whatever form, they'd keep fighting. Because they'd built real lives—with love and loss and right and wrong and hope. Real, life-changing hope.

Everything Elijah and Ace had was a delusion. It made them dangerous, sure, but it didn't have to rule their lives. If every time Wyatts and Knights came together they fought for right and good, well, that was life.

As long as they built one.

"Do you think…" Cecilia leaned close to his ear, eyeing the men who were still going through the rubble. "Do you think Tucker's part of Cody's old group and that's why he's being so weird?"

"It seems possible. We can't say anything, though. They kicked Cody out once other people knew he was part of the group. If Tucker is working with them, we have to keep quiet."

Cecilia nodded once, then rested her head against his shoulder. "We're okay," she murmured, as if she had to say it out loud to believe it.

It was odd. He was in an unreasonable amount of pain, bleeding profusely, and she wasn't doing much better. Bloody and banged up, sitting in the middle of the Badlands with the afternoon sun beating down.

But he felt…right. Like the things that had been all wrong for the past few months, all that gray and frustration and anxiety had lifted.

The Sons still existed, Ace and Elijah were both alive—if in jail. But even in the face of that, Jamison and Cody had reunited with their first loves. Cody had a daughter, Jamison had Liza's young half sister looking up to him like a father figure, and Gage and Felicity were getting married and starting a family.

And Brady Wyatt had at some point fallen in love with Cecilia. Who didn't care so much about right or wrong, but did what she had to do. Who fought, tooth and nail, for the people she loved.

What wasn't to love about that? "I love you," he murmured into her dusty hair.

"Sure you're not dying?" she joked. Or half joked. He could feel the anxiety radiating off her.

But he was going to be just fine.

Epilogue

Two weeks later

Cecilia sat in Grandma Pauline's kitchen. It was a full house these days. Sarah and Rachel were staying here while the Knight house was repaired from the fire. Duke had insisted on staying on the property, and no one could get through to Duke when he had an idea in his head.

Cecilia had been forced to stay at Grandma Pauline's once she'd been released from the hospital, and so had Brady. Everyone had been surprised when Cecilia insisted they share a room, but people seemed to be getting used to their new normal.

Well, not Brady, who was back to being surly as he recovered. The gunshot wound to his leg had been serious, and though it hadn't shattered any bone it had done some damage that would take considerable time to heal.

Having to accept help to get around did *not* make for a happy Wyatt, but he was the one who'd come up with their current plan. If she hadn't already been in love with him, she would have fallen for him when he'd suggested it.

The door opened, and Jamison stepped inside, gesturing Layla to follow him. She looked nervous, but better than she'd been in the hospital.

Cecilia immediately got up and went to gather Layla into a hug. Layla squeezed back, sniffling into Cecilia's shoulder. "I wasn't sure I wanted to come, but I knew you'd come get me if I didn't. And you need your rest." Layla pulled away. "Where is he?"

Cecilia nodded thanks at Jamison who slipped away. "I can't hold him yet because of my injuries, so he's upstairs being spoiled. Jamison will go get him, but I wanted to talk to you about something first."

"I know. I can't have him back. I… I feel better, but I can't—"

Cecilia kept her hands on her friend's arms. "I think you can. But you don't have to, Layla. You've got to do what's right for you, first and foremost."

"The state can't take him, Cecilia. And when Elijah gets out of jail—"

Cecilia led Layla to the table and made her sit down. "We're going to protect you and Mak from Elijah. Always. Never worry about that."

"I lost my job. My therapist said I'm doing better, but—"

"But it's hard. You've been through *a lot*." Cecilia took her friend's hands in hers. "You should be around your son. You should have work that allows you to do that. And you should feel safe."

"I don't—"

"I'm going to offer something, and I want you to understand it was the Wyatts' idea. I didn't have anything to do with it, so don't feel like you have to take it because you owe me."

"I owe you my life. I owe everyone…"

"Layla."

She sucked in a deep breath and nodded. "I know. You're my best friend and I would have done the same for you. I'm just…fragile, Cecilia. I don't feel strong enough for anything." She winced. "My therapist says it's good to tell people that, but it feels awful."

"Which is why we want you to move in here. We've got two people recovering from major injuries. The Wyatt brothers come and go with their families in tow. Grandma Pauline is…well, let's just say everything she has to do for this big house and ranch is a lot for a woman her age." Cecilia prayed to God Pauline didn't hear that one. "She could use help. Live-in help. You'd work for her, be part of taking care of your son, and those of us hobbling around until we're better. It can be temporary until you feel well enough to look for a new job, and live on your own. Or it can be permanent."

"But…" Layla blinked, tears filling her eyes. "That's too good to be true."

Cecilia smiled, squeezing Layla's hands. "The

Wyatts are a little too good to be true sometimes. It's easier if you just accept it, not question if you deserve it. So, what do you think?"

Layla hesitated. "What about when you and Brady are better and go back to your real lives? Will Pauline really need my help? Will Mak have…stability, you know?"

Cecilia blinked. She hadn't been thinking about when she and Brady were better. At all. She cleared her throat, trying to hide her uncertainty from Layla. "Well, Pauline will still need help. And Brady and I come out here all the time. We wouldn't just abandon Mak."

Layla's eyebrows drew together. "His own mother did."

"No. His own mother got sick, and now she's doing better. And she has a whole village who wants to take care of her and her son. Mak's very lucky."

"I…" She sucked in a deep breath. "I can't say no, can I? It would be…it'd be stupid to say no." Layla abruptly got to her feet. Cecilia turned in her chair. Pauline had brought in Mak and Layla was crying over him.

Cecilia smiled at Grandma Pauline, but Layla's words were rattling around in her head. *What about when you and Brady are better?*

"Why don't you take him into the living room, sweetheart. Let me show you," Grandma Pauline said, ushering a crying Layla holding a babbling Mak into the living room. "We'll give you a few minutes of privacy, huh?"

Layla sniffled and nodded and disappeared into the room. Cecilia stood alone in the kitchen.

What about when you and Brady are better?

No, she wouldn't sit around worrying over that question. She went to her and Brady's makeshift room and found him lying on the bed, reading a book.

"What about when we're better?" she demanded with no preamble. She didn't know why she felt so… angry. So shaky. But they hadn't discussed this. Why hadn't it even come up?

Brady looked up from his book. "Huh?"

"What's going to happen when we're better?"

He blinked then, shifted in the bed. "Well…" He cleared his throat. "I'm not sure what you're asking me, Cecilia."

"Where are we going to go? Are you going back to your apartment and I'm going back to the rez? Does this continue?" She gestured between them. "What are we *doing*?"

He set the book aside. "I'm not going to have this conversation with you standing there, acting like you're accusing me of something. Come sit down."

"Oh, don't use that high-handed tone to boss me around."

He raised an eyebrow. He had a tendency to do that and make her feel like an idiot for wanting to stomp her foot and yell.

She plopped herself on the bed next to him because she *was* reasonable, even if it felt like one simple sentence had sent her a little off the deep end. Then he wrapped his arm around her, pulling her close until she rested her head on his shoulder.

"Once you're back to work, you'll want to stay on the rez," he said rationally.

"I guess so."

"I don't have to live in the county, and it's not like it's too far to drive every day."

She sat up straight, something like panic beating through her. "Are you suggesting you move in with me?"

"Isn't that what *you're* getting at?"

"No… Well, sort of. I mean, we're basically living together now. Just with a grandma hovering around."

"Exactly."

"I…"

"Alternatively, we could stay here and both commute when we're reinstated. Or I could just stay here, and you could live on the rez. Commute will suck, but I'm not going to be able to deal with those stairs at my apartment for a long while yet. Hell, I'm half convinced to just give up my badge."

She pulled out of his grasp, outraged. "You can't do that."

"Why not? I've been out for months. I'll be out for longer now. Why go back?"

She shook her head. She knew he was tired of being hurt. Tired of not working, but he couldn't honestly be thinking about quitting. "Because you love it."

He was quiet for a while. "I guess I do." He squeezed her close. "I think the point, Cecilia, is that we'll work out whatever we do next together."

She tipped her head up to look at him. Life was funny. She'd always looked up to Brady. Always been in a certain amount of awe of him, even when he was irritating her to death. She wouldn't have admitted it. Even at New Year's Eve, kissing him, she hadn't admitted she had *this* inside of her.

It had taken fear. Struggle. Now, she wouldn't stop admitting it. Her pride wasn't as important as being honest with him.

"You're a pretty good guy, Wyatt."

"Yeah, yeah. What did Layla say?"

"She's going to do it."

"Good. You know, it wouldn't be so bad. Staying here. Helping Grandma and Dev out. Keeping close to Mak. I wouldn't mind it so much."

Cecilia settled back against his chest. "No, I wouldn't mind it either."

This was not ever what she'd planned for her life. A guy like Brady. Living this close to home. Having her best friend and her best friend's baby under one roof. It wasn't a normal family by any stretch, but she'd never had *normal*.

What she'd had was love, and now she had more of it.

She settled into Brady and sighed. "I love you,"

she murmured. Because no matter what happened, love was always the reason you gutted through, fought for what you had to, and most of all, survived.

* * * * *

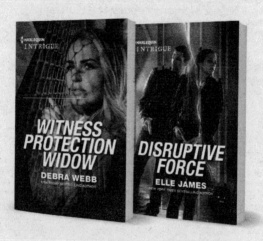

After very little sleep and an early call from his father the next
morning, Brick dressed in his uniform and drove down to the law
enforcement building. He was hoping that this would be the day
that his father, Marshal Hud Savage, told him he would finally be
on active duty. He couldn't wait to get his teeth into something, a
real investigation. After finding that woman last night, he wanted
more than anything to be the one to get her justice.

"Come in and close the door," his father said before motioning
him into a chair across from his desk.

"Is this about the woman I encountered last night?" he asked
as he removed his Stetson and dropped into a chair across from
his father. He'd stayed at the hospital until the doctor had sent him
home. When he called this morning, he'd been told that the woman
appeared to be in a catatonic state and was unresponsive.

"We have a name on your Jane Doe," his father said now.
"Natalie Berkshire."

Brick frowned. The name sounded vaguely familiar. But that
wasn't what surprised him. "Already? Her fingerprints?"

Hud nodded and slid a copy of the *Billings Gazette* toward him.
He picked it up and saw the headline sprawled across the front
page, "Alleged Infant Killer Released for Lack of Evidence." The
newspaper was two weeks old.

Brick felt a jolt rock him back in his chair. "She's that woman?" He couldn't help his shock. He thought of the terrified woman who'd crossed in front of his truck last night. She was nothing like the woman he remembered seeing on television coming out of the law enforcement building in Billings after being released.

"I don't know what to say." Nor did he know what to think. The woman he'd found had definitely been victimized. He thought he'd saved her. He'd been hell-bent on getting her justice. With his Stetson balanced on his knee, he raked his fingers through his hair.

"I'm trying to make sense of this, as well," his father said. "Since her release, more evidence had come out in former cases. She's now wanted for questioning in more deaths of patients who'd been under her care from not just Montana. Apparently, the moment she was released, she disappeared. Billings PD checked her apartment. It appeared that she'd left in a hurry and hasn't been seen since."

"Until last night when she stumbled in front of my pickup," Brick said. "You think she's been held captive all this time?"

"Looks that way," Hud said. "We found her older-model sedan parked behind the convenience store down on Highway 191. We're assuming she'd stopped for gas. The attendant who was on duty recognized her from a photo. She remembered seeing Natalie at the gas pumps and thinking she looked familiar but couldn't place her at the time. The attendant said a large motor home pulled in and she lost sight of her and didn't see her again."

"When was this?" Brick asked.

"Two weeks ago. Both the back seat and the trunk of her car were full of her belongings."

"So she was running away when she was abducted." Brick couldn't really blame her. "After all the bad publicity, I can see where she couldn't stay in Billings. But taking off like that makes her either look guilty—or scared."

"Or both."

Don't miss
Double Action Deputy *by B.J. Daniels,*
available July 2020 wherever
Harlequin Intrigue books and ebooks are sold.

Harlequin.com

HIEXP0620

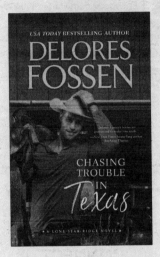

Love Harlequin romance?

DISCOVER.

Be the first to find out about promotions, news and exclusive content!

Facebook.com/HarlequinBooks

Twitter.com/HarlequinBooks

Instagram.com/HarlequinBooks

Pinterest.com/HarlequinBooks

ReaderService.com

EXPLORE.

Sign up for the Harlequin e-newsletter and download a free book from any series at **TryHarlequin.com**

CONNECT.

Join our Harlequin community to share your thoughts and connect with other romance readers! **Facebook.com/groups/HarlequinConnection**

HSOCIAL2020